M

BROTHER
TO
GALAHAD

BROTHER TO GALAHAD

by Gwendolyn Bowers

illustrated by Don Bolognese

New York *Henry Z. Walck, Inc.* *1963*

For George Ellery Washburn
"a verray parfit gentil knight"

Contents

BROTHER
TO
GALAHAD

At the Beginning

WHEN THE ROMAN LEGIONS sailed away from Britain, there was tumult and fighting in the land. Wild chieftains from the north swept over Hadrian's Wall to destroy the Roman towns, and barons and nobles seized the fortified places and strove with each other for power, because Vortigern, King of the Britons, was old and ill, and had no son to be King after him. And because he was too feeble to check the strife in his land, Vortigern sent over the sea to Hengist and Horsa for help. They came in their long boats bringing the Germanic hordes, and they swarmed over the land intending to possess it for themselves. Then the fighting grew even fiercer, the men of Britain against the invaders, until Uther Pendragon, Vortigern's warrior, put them to flight after many battles. And when Vortigern died, men chose Uther for their king. But the nobles still strengthened their forts and built their castles and watchtowers, and strove for power among themselves, until Arthur came from Tintagel and drew the sword from the stone, and proved his kingship, and brought peace to the land.

And Arthur married the Lady Guinevere, daughter of King Leodogrance, and held splendid court at Camelot. Merlin the Enchanter gave him wise counsel, and the bard Taliessin sang of his mighty deeds, and his fame spread across the seas. Kings paid him truage, and the greatest knights of Christendom came to offer him fealty. Some of them had lands and castles of their own, so that they were considered as kings in their own lands; some were kings' sons, like Sir Launcelot and his brother Bors; but some were poor young men of noble birth, who came and served humbly, and waited for a chance to prove their worth and earn knighthood.

In the banqueting hall at Camelot stood the Round Table of King Arthur. Some said he had ordered it so made that all the company might sit down in equal honor. Others said it was the table of the Last Supper, come down from Joseph of Arimathea to King Leodogrance, and given by him as a marriage gift to the Lady Guinevere. A hundred and fifty knights sat down at that table together—the goodliest fellowship of knights the world has ever seen. Each knight had the device of his shield blazoned on the back of his chair in gold or argent laid with rich colors, and his banner hung from the wall above his place. But one chair stood always empty, covered with cloth of white samite fringed with gold. Men called it the Siege Perilous, and no knight, however hardy, dared to raise the covering or sit in that place.

In all the fellowship of the Round Table, no others equaled in prowess Sir Launcelot of the Lake, nor Tristram of Lyonnesse; none surpassed in courtliness and chivalry Sir Gawain, nephew to the King. Men said many of the great knights were kinsmen, though far removed, descended from Joseph of Arimathea, who came to Glaston long ago, bringing the Holy Grail.

Over the stone-bright roads from Camelot rode the mail-clad knights who kept the King's peace; lone knights-errant pursued their solitary quests—to keep a vow or right a wrong. Along the hedgerows and into the fields of May rode ladies in white and green, and page boys bright as butterflies, to gather hyacinths and cowslips and boughs of the blossoming thorn.

And pilgrims walked the way to Glaston to see the Holy Spring and the miraculous Thorn, and to pray in the Abbey that men raised to mark the holy place.

1

Hugh of Alleyn

ON THE WELSH COAST, facing the wash of the steel-cold sea, the battlements of an ancient castle rose out of the morning mists. In an older time it had been a rude fort with long walls facing the sea. Now grim towers buttressed its four corners and stately battlements rose above the barbican that guarded the approach from the moat. Beyond the iron-spiked door, crumbling passageways connected the four towers, and triangular stone stairs spiraled upward around a center post like the flutings of a fan, and gave access to the chambers above. Weapons were stacked in the keep below the great hall, and shields and tattered battle flags hung from the walls, but no flag whipped from the battlements, and no men at arms rode over the drawbridge. Only an ancient coat of arms, a shield of white limestone quartered in red, proclaimed the castle to be the ancient fortress of Brannlyr, long held by the knights of Alleyn.

In a tower room facing the sea, young Hugh of Alleyn was up and ready for the day, though the torch had barely glimmered out in its iron bracket above the stair. He wore a rust-colored tunic belted in leather,

and he had the dark hair and blue eyes of the Cymri.
He leaned against the wedge-shaped stone that shielded
the narrow embrasure, his thumbs hooked into his belt
and his eyes squinted toward a strip of pale glittering
light below the tattered edges of the rising mist. He
was sure there was something out there, a bobbing dark
speck—a sea creature, perhaps, a seal or a great fish,
not unknown to the crags of Brannlyr, but not common, either.

A serving woman entered the room, carrying a
pile of folded garments. When she saw Hugh she
stopped and watched him with a troubled look.

"Moira," he said without turning, "there's something out there, in that white strip. Can you tell what
it is?"

She caught her breath and raised her hand as
though to ward off the evil eye. "No, no, young master,
nor look you either," she whispered fearfully. "It is not
for mortals to spy upon the spirits in the mists and waters
of Brannlyr! Come you away from the window until
the sun gives the world back to men."

Hugh turned from the window then and laughed.
"What nonsense you brought with you from that pagan
island of yours," he jested. "You know middle earth
belongs to men, and from far-off times Brannlyr has
belonged to the lords of Alleyn." He spoke the last
with a touch of pride.

"My people remember that from the beginning it was the dwelling place of Bran the Blessed, and Lyr, the god of the shades," she said, her fear making her bolder. "Sorrow comes to men who dare to dwell among the shades, as your lady mother knows."

"My lady mother still grieves for the death of my father, as does all his household," Hugh said sternly, with all the laughter gone out of his eyes. "Do you not trouble her with this nonsense too."

Moira looked at the tall serious lad before her, and saw how he had the look of his father, and she thought for the first time that he was a child no longer; he was now lord of Alleyn. She moved her head in awkward deference and carried her bundle to the carved wardrobe chest that served as a bench by the fireplace. When she had shut the lid she hurried out again without speaking.

Hugh felt some of the pleasure go out of the morning with the calling up of his mother's long grief and the dim memory of the night flight from the safety of his mother's old home to Brannlyr, where his father lay wounded, and of his own loss that kept him at his mother's side when he should be page and squire in a knight's household.

For afterward the lady Blanche would not leave the fortress where her lord had died, but shut herself up in her tower room and let the flags be lowered from the battlements, and forbade all jousting and shows of arms in the courtyard. The child Hugh was left to go wandering and unnoticed about the crumbling recesses of the ancient place until he met an adventure that stayed with him for a long time, and brought him back to his mother's thought.

He had lost his way in a maze of crumbling passageways and blind turnings and come upon a heavy door partly open, where a ray of light flickered and glowed red in the dark. He tried to peer in, and would have entered, when a short twisted creature, with arms and legs all awry, suddenly stepped out, closed the door behind him, and stood looking down at Hugh. His mouth was fixed in a grin, and one eye was closed by a long scar, and his look was so fearful that the child started away in terror, only to trip and fall screaming onto a pile of rubble. Then the creature picked him up and gave him to a man who brought him, sobbing with fright, to Moira. She hushed his crying and tucked him in his bed, and his mother came and sat by him until he fell asleep. But when he tried to tell her what had befallen him, she looked stern and pale, and said the creature was no goblin but a man who had served them well, and she charged Moira to see that Hugh did not wander into the ancient crypts again. Now all that was years ago, and if it came to his mind at all, it was like a half-remembered dream.

From that time Moira looked after him until he was old enough to look after himself. For all that Moira took him to the dim-lit chapel with his lady mother, and spoke the holy words with them, she kept something old and pagan in her deeper mind, and when the winter fogs closed down on Brannlyr she remembered the tales of her people. Then she looked over the steel-cold sea and spoke of the water-spirits—Lyr and Finn Lug and Bran the Blessed—and she told of their magic possessions: of the shining Cup of Truth that broke when three lies were told; of the magic Cauldron that could feed a multitude and never be empty; and of the terrible Luin, the spear that so thirsted for battle it would smoke and burst into flames. She told of Caer Sidi, the Turning Island, where Avallach, Prince of the Evening, ruled over the marshes and tors of Avalon. On winter nights the dark came early, and when Moira had drawn up Hugh's coverlet of golden fox skins and closed his bed curtains, she would sit by the fire, and he would hear her wordless singing threading through the night sounds, rising and falling away, mingled with the moaning of the wind and the tide.

Hugh outgrew Moira's tales when Owain, keeper of the horse, chose a mount for him, and Dickon the groom taught him to ride. Freed from Moira's watchful eye, Hugh gave no thought to the rubble-choked ruins he had explored as a child, for his world was no longer bounded by the castle walls. Dickon's Tam, a hearty, red-faced lad, tamed a hunting hawk for him, and the two boys rode the heath and forests of Brannlyr day after day. When Hugh was nearly ten, the lady Blanche perceived that her son was growing tall and took thought to his education. She instructed Herlewin the Chaplain to give him lessons in Latin and French, and to these she added training in courtesy; but because her lord had died in battle and her son was dear to her, she suffered no one to teach him the use of arms.

When Hugh turned back to the window the fog had thinned and the dark speck was nearer. It was not a sea creature after all, but a fisherman's coracle, a small boat of hides stretched over a light frame. As Hugh watched, the man beached the boat and lifted out a string of fish. He turned the boat over his head like a basket and began to climb the slope where the ascent was easiest. He wore a coarse dark robe with the back edge of it drawn forward between his legs and tucked into a rope belt. His arms and legs were brown and muscular, and he moved with the ease of a young man.

"It is Brian the hermit," Hugh said, and he watched until the man passed out of sight close to the wall.

Hugh knew that as Brian went among the stone houses clustered outside the castle wall he would give his fish away, as he gave the cabbages and lentils from his garden patch, until only the smallest and poorest were left for himself. No one in the village knew where Brian came from; for a year he had been living in a forest shelter he contrived among the ruins of an ancient stonework. If the villagers thought it strange that a young, able-bodied man should choose the poverty and solitude of a hermit, they did not trouble him with questions. They knew him for a good man and they called him Brother Brian.

Hugh turned slowly away from the window, remembering that on this morning he was expected to read French with his lady mother, and after that, Latin with Herlewin. The best part of the day would be over, he thought, before he could get to more important things. He went down the spiraling stair to the cobbled passage outside, hoping to find Tam and plan for some fishing when lessons were over.

In the shops and castle kitchens the day's work was already underway. Through the chill damp air came the clink of hammers on metal and the smell of baking bread. Gillian the milkmaid crossed the courtyard with a brimming pail. A green-eyed tiger cat rubbed against her ankles, arching its back and eyeing the pail hungrily. Gillian bobbed a curtsy to Hugh, and the rim of yellow cream slid up and over the edge. The cat fell to work with greedy tongue. A goose straying from the poultry yard curved its neck like a feathered snake and hissed at the cat. A rough-coated terrier raced

across the cobbles, yelping a challenge to both his enemies. The cat stiffened and bristled and flailed out with
her claws. Gillian set down her pail with a thump, and
more cream slopped on the ground. The dairy mistress
hurried out puffing and scolding. With a sweep of her
arm she boxed Gillian's ears, scattered the animals, and
rescued the pail.

Hugh laughed and went on, keeping a lookout for
Tam until the warm bread smell reminded him that he
was hungry. He gave over his search and pushed open
the door to the castle kitchens. Otho the Butler would
give him a wedge of new bread with a slice of last
night's venison and a flagon of milk.

After his breakfast Hugh climbed the spiraling stair
again, thinking enviously of Tam, free to ride off with
neither French nor Latin to trouble his brains. Not that
Hugh minded reading his Latin—it sounded the way it
looked on the page. But French was another thing.
After four years of trying, Hugh still couldn't shape
his tongue to it. But he greeted his mother courteously
and sat himself down with his book, pronouncing the
words carefully to please her. He had read scarcely a
page when Herlewin the Chaplain came to tell the lady
Blanche that a stranger had arrived and asked the hospitality of the castle.

"He must be a scholar, my lady," Herlewin said,
"for he carried an open book in his hand—methinks

'twas Latin—as though he perused it by the way, and he spoke in excellent French."

"A scholar? Then he is welcome. Bid Otho serve him a meal in the hall, and do you, good Herlewin, share it with him for courtesy's sake," the lady said, for it was not her custom to sit down with a chance guest.

Few travelers came to Brannlyr, and Hugh was eager to give over his halting French to see this one; even a gray-bearded scholar might have an interesting tale to tell. Herlewin saw the lad's eagerness and said gravely, "My lady, since the stranger appears to be a learned man and discourses in the French tongue, it might profit Hugh here . . ."

"Well bethought," the lady said. "Hugh, go with Herlewin and welcome this scholar. Sit at the board with them and listen to his discourse. If he speaks to you, answer him in French. And whatever of wisdom he speaks, heed it to your profit."

Hugh went swiftly out to the courtyard and saw a young man on a chestnut courser, and he held a book in his hand. His face was weathered, and his eyes and pointed beard were brown. He wore a cloak of rich blue called pers over a shirt of chain mail. His saddle and bridle were of Spanish leather, unornamented save for a pair of cunningly wrought silver wings that swept upward past the horse's ears. A sleek greyhound pranced about the horse on delicate feet, and stretched his slim head toward his master's stirrup and begged him to dismount. The stranger introduced himself as Leormand of Brittany.

Later, in the hall, Hugh listened obediently to his discourse, and though it was in excellent French, it was not as scholarly as the lady Blanche would have wished.

Leormand's book lay by him on the table. When Herlewin questioned him concerning it, he said it was Latin—an account of Caesar's wars against the Gauls. The knight had made a long study of it and accounted Caesar a great *dux bellorum.*

Hugh understood the Latin and said, "Leader of wars."

Leormand looked his way and smiled. "Caesar carried war into many lands and conquered many peoples, and brought slaves and treasure back to Rome," he said. "For that the books praise him, and they praise his Romans because they built roads and fortresses and gave people the law."

Herlewin nodded gravely. "Brannlyr was once a Roman fortress," he said. "Commanding both seaward and landward approaches as it does, it has ever been a valued defense for this island. The first Romans built on a native earthwork. Four hundred years they held it, and when the oldest parts weakened they tore them down and used the stone to build anew. So they en-

larged the walls and added living quarters for the com-
manders. Since the Romans left, the knights of Alleyn
have possessed Brannlyr; it has been their dwelling as
well as their fortress."

Leormand nodded. "Caesar's empire has fallen to
ruin," he said, "and lands that once bowed to Caesar
now pay truage to Arthur."

"Arthur is no Caesar," Herlewin said quickly. "He
does not enslave the people. He gives them justice, and
they live at peace under the law."

Leormand nodded his agreement. "Therefore his
fame has grown so great across the Channel that France's
greatest knight, Launcelot du Lac, left his stronghold of
Benwick to serve King Arthur at Camelot. Now I
journey thither to see this king whom men call greater
than Caesar, the king who numbers the noblest knights
of the world in his fellowship of the Round Table."

Enthusiasm sparked in the knight's dark eyes, and
his hands moved in quick gestures as he talked of the
prowess of Sir Launcelot and his friend Tristram of
Lyonnesse, of Bors and Bedivere and Percivale of Wales.
Leormand was aware that Hugh was listening eagerly,
and he turned to him with a smile. "The children of
Brittany learn of Arthur in their cradles," he said. "As
soon as they can run about their chief sport is to enact
the great feat of Arthur's youth, when he hunted the
boar with the silver bristles, the Twrch Trwyth that

was killing the cattle, and pursued him through all Ireland and Scotland down into Wales, and drove him at last into the Severn Sea. Because of that great hunt I mean to offer my greyhound to the King, and pay him my respects, and then I shall return and tell my people I have seen King Arthur."

Thus did the stranger entertain them with tales, and Hugh heeded every word as he had been bidden. Never in his memory had he heard such manly talk in the hall, nor heard such marvelous tales of the King, nor had he ever seen a knight like Leormand. When the stranger rose to take his rest, Hugh would fain have heard more. Even so, he knew that in truth he had learned much to his profit.

2

Merlin the Enchanter

WHEN LEORMAND RODE OUT of the courtyard Hugh was there to see him go. Hugh asked him, "How far is it to Camelot?"

Leormand looked at Hugh, then his eyes twinkled and his white teeth glinted through his laughter. "I'll wager it is nearer than you think," he said.

Then he was off on his winged horse with the greyhound prancing before him, and Hugh turned back to find his own world suddenly grown too small. He knew that riding and fishing and lessons with Herlewin could no longer fill his days. All that night he dreamed of a boar hunt; he followed it mile after mile. The next morning he tried to tell Tam that King Arthur was greater than Caesar, but Tam had not heard of Caesar. He listened respectfully when Hugh told of Launcelot and Tristram, but it was the boar hunt he took most note of. After that Hugh talked no more of knighthood, but he never ceased to think of it.

One morning when Hugh was minded to go fishing, he walked outside the wall in search of Tam. He followed a forest path where he and Tam had ridden many a time. At a fork in the hazel copse he took a turning along a way he had not traveled before. At the end of the hazel wood there seemed to be a falling away of the earth, and the path suddenly plunged below the overhanging rocks into a sunless chasm where no leaf stirred and no bird sang. From below the outcropping rock came the rush and fall of a hidden stream. Age-old trees slanted through the low-hanging mist, their leaves grown dark and lush in the chill dampness. Interweaving branches shut out the light and sounds of middle earth, and save for the rush of unseen water, all was cold green silence.

Hugh had gone but a little way when he began to feel a listening in the silence, and a watching in the shadows, and it seemed to him that he walked in an unearthly place. Then he would have turned back, but a man was coming toward him in the gloom. His cloak and doublet were black, lined and edged with green. His gaze was compelling, even a distance away, and when he came closer Hugh saw his mismatched eyes—one brown and one green. Their look was full of old wisdom and knowledge of things yet to be, and Hugh was suddenly afraid. Without his knowing, his hand moved in Moira's sign against the evil eye.

The shadow of a smile crossed the man's face. "Hugh of Alleyn," he said, "when you return to the world of men, give over your thought of fishing and go

instead to the hermit in the forest of Brannlyr. Say to
him that one whose life he despaired of is recovered
from his wound and whole again."

And while Hugh stood silent in astonishment, for
he had in truth had fishing in mind, the man turned back
and was lost in the mist and the gloom. So great had
been his air of authority that Hugh had no thought but
to do his bidding. He turned back toward the forest of
Brannlyr.

Brother Brian was at work in his garden beyond
the cairn of ancient stones when he saw the young lord

of the castle waiting uncertainly by the empty hut. He left his work and came across the field.

"Welcome to the lord of Alleyn," he said, and his manner was grave and courteous, but not humble. He offered Hugh a bench in the shade, and from a stone grotto over the spring he brought flagons of barley water mingled with vinegar and honey. Sipping the cool drink with the sunlight around him and the drone of bees coming from the plaited straw hives, Hugh could scarce recall the fearsome landscape of the morning.

So when it came time for him to speak, Hugh only said, "I met a man who bade me tell you that one whose life you despaired of has recovered of his wound and is whole again."

A look of joy lighted the hermit's face, yet like one who fears to believe the thing he wants most to hear, he begged Hugh to tell all the tale.

Then the remembrance of it came clearer to Hugh, and he told of the gloomy chasm with the invisible rushing water, and of the stranger in black and green, and of how the stranger spoke Hugh's name and knew his thoughts.

"And was his countenance like that of other men?" Brian asked eagerly. Then Hugh told of his mismatched eyes.

When he heard that, Brian said joyfully, "Now

you have brought me the gladdest news I have heard in many a month."

"Who then was the stranger?" Hugh asked.

Brian answered, "He is called Merlin."

Then Hugh remembered tales he had heard—of how Merlin raised the monoliths of Stonehenge that men called the Giants' Dance, and brought a dragon out of a stone that was at the bottom of a lake, and foretold the coming of King Arthur and many other wonders. And Hugh asked eagerly, "Is he in truth an enchanter?"

Brian laughed and said, "Of that I know nothing, only that he gives the King wise counsel; his wisdom surpasses that of ordinary men, and so they call him Merlin the Enchanter."

Now Brian's eyes were merry and young, and when he spoke of Merlin and King Arthur his voice was eager, and Hugh knew he was no true hermit. And because Hugh dreamed much of many-towered Camelot, and said over to himself the names of Launcelot and Bors and Bedivere, and longed above all things to see a tournament, he could not forbear to ask Brian another question: "Were you of King Arthur's court?"

And Brian said humbly, "I was the least of that great company, for I had just won my spurs, and I was full of overweening pride. In the tourney I sought to win praise for myself, and in my foolhardiness I wounded a brother knight so that he was near to death. And though no one blamed me, I knew I was guilty of his hurt; so I quit the court and took upon me the life of a hermit, and vowed never to enter the lists nor seek worship at arms unless he should be made whole again."

"And now if he be whole, will you go back to Camelot?" Hugh asked.

"First I must journey to Avalon," Brian said slowly, as though he were thinking aloud.

"To Avalon?" Hugh repeated in a hushed tone.

Brian smiled. "That is the old name. Now it is called Glaston, and men have built a great Abbey there to mark the place where Joseph of Arimathea built a little church when he came bringing the Holy Grail to Britain. I shall ask the brothers of the Abbey to let me dwell a day among them and give thanks. . . ." Then Brother Brian was silent, and Hugh knew that for courtesy's sake he should not question him further. So he finished his barley drink and took his leave, and went back to Brannlyr thinking of Camelot and Glaston and the Grail.

That night Hugh and his lady mother sat at table in the great hall. Otho the Butler stood by, and serving men carved the meat and served the meal; but the long table was empty, save for Bronwen, the lady Blanche's gentlewoman, who sat a little apart. Hugh looked down the oaken board and thought how it would be if his father still lived. He would have men at arms about him, and retainers to sit below the salt, and there would be talk of battles and tournaments and knightly deeds. But Hugh himself might not be there, for he would be sent to be page and squire in some noble household, perhaps even to many-towered Camelot. He fell to imagining what it might be like in Arthur's hall, and he felt that he would gladly be a serving man there if he could but see the glorious company assembled, and hear the tales told at the Table Round.

Hugh looked at his lady mother, sitting pale and silent with her old grief still upon her, and he wondered if he dared speak his thoughts to her. So he began, "My lady mother, as I walked in the wood today I met Merlin the Enchanter, and he spoke my name!"

"My son!" The lady started so that her slender hand sent a silver goblet unheeded to the floor. "What did he tell you?"

"He bade me carry a message to the hermit of Brannlyr—that one who was wounded is now whole again," Hugh answered.

"And what more? Did he speak of Brannlyr and of things to come?" the lady asked.

"No more," said Hugh, "but I went to the hermit as he bade me, and . . ." Then Hugh saw that his mother had returned to her own thoughts and he left off his tale, because he knew she would take no pleasure in his imaginings.

"What is the hermit called?" she asked after a little.

"The village folk name him Brother Brian," Hugh answered.

"I did not know of a hermit at Brannlyr, and we have sent no alms," she said in a gentle, troubled tone. "Otho, let two loaves and a dole of flesh or fowl be sent to the hermit each day."

And Hugh thought suddenly that he must talk with Brian again before he left the forest of Brannlyr, and he said, "Mother, let me carry the dole to Brother Brian."

And because she supposed all hermits to be old and holy men, with no care for feats of arms, the lady Blanche gave willing assent.

3

The Greatest Wonder of Britain

THE NEXT MORNING as Hugh was leaving the courtyard with the hermit's dole of bread and roasted fowl, he came upon Tam, the groom's son, plaiting a bridle by the stables. Tam left off work and jumped to his feet.

"My father has ordered me to bring in a pair of colts from the outer field, but if it should be your wish to go fishing today, I will tell him and he will send another," Tam said hopefully. "I have plaited a strong net and lashed it to an iron hoop that Gwillim made at the forge, and set a handle to it, and we could try for the fighting salmon we lost last time."

"It must wait for another day, Tam," Hugh said, impatient to be off. "Bring my horse."

He mounted, and cantered through a crumbling gate to the village road. The dark stone houses of Brannlyr clustered in the shelter of its castle walls, and followed the jagged road down the cliffside to the market square. The road was already alive with the business of the morning; the villagers were driving their animals and trundling their handcarts to market. Goosegirls and dairymaids bobbed Hugh a good day; gray-smocked countrymen touched their forelocks respectfully, for he was the young master and they wished him well. But some, who remembered earlier strife, wondered uneasily why the young lord was always about the village instead of learning skill at arms; for who else was left to order the defenses of the castle and its village, if the need should arise?

Hugh followed the road beyond the Market Cross, where it dwindled to a rough cart track and lost itself in the forest. When he came to Brian's hut, Hugh was suddenly abashed to offer a dole of bread and fowl, for he knew that Brian was not in truth a poor hermit, but a knight of King Arthur's court. But Brian received it graciously and spoke his thanks. "One loaf will suffice until I go to Glastonbury," he said. "The rest I will give to the poor, for yesterday my catch of fish was all too small."

"In truth, I came mostly for this," Hugh said, "to ask you of courtesy to tell me, before you go, somewhat of King Arthur's court, and of Glaston, and of the Holy Grail."

Brian smiled and said, "No man could tell it all, for I believe no court in the world matches the splendor of King Arthur's, and no knights equal in prowess Sir Tristram and Launcelot of the Lake; Glastonbury is holy and full of ancient mystery, but the Holy Grail is the greatest wonder of Britain. and the Quest of the Holy

Grail will be the greatest adventure that any knight may have in this world."

"Then I pray you, tell me first of the Holy Grail," Hugh said.

So Brian brought flagons of cool barley water from the spring, and when they had seated themselves by the droning hives, he began the tale.

"In the early days, while the Romans were still in Britain, Joseph of Arimathea came from the Holy Land with twelve of his followers, bringing the Cup of the Last Supper, which men afterward called the Holy Grail. And Joseph journeyed with his company through Britain until they came to a place where a high tor rose out of a marshy plain, and wild apples grew along the glassy stream that circled it. In the old time men called the place Avalon. . . ."

"The place of Caer Sidi, the Turning Island," Hugh added, catching his breath.

Brian looked at him in surprise. "So men called it in the old time," he said, "but now they name it Glaston, as I told you. There Joseph built a little church of rushes, round like a beehive, in the place where the great Abbey now stands. Around the church they built twelve huts in a circle, one for each of Joseph's companions. And Joseph preached to the people of Britain and to kings and chieftains of the old pagan time, and he did many wonders because of the miraculous powers of the Grail. One of the wonders was this: he set his staff into the ground and it took root and grew, leaf and branch, until it became a thorn tree. To this day it flourishes by the Abbey, and bears its flowers in winter. Pilgrims still journey to Glaston to see the Holy Thorn."

Hugh thought on the wonder of a winter-blossoming tree. Then he asked, "And what of the Grail?"

"It is a great mystery, and I cannot tell it of my own knowledge, nor can any man," Brian answered; "but men talked of it when I was page and squire in Arthur's court, for the knights of the Round Table claim kinship with Joseph of Arimathea, and hold him in great reverence. And the tale they told was this: Before Joseph died he entrusted the keeping of the Grail to his sons, and to their sons after them. But he foretold that in after years men would grow heedless of the holy teaching, and the Grail would vanish from their sight until the coming of a knight worthy to behold it. He should be a knight of Joseph's line, perfect in honor and courage and charity. Then Joseph took a white shield and marked it with a cross of his own blood, and said it would remain bright forever. No man should bear the Red Cross shield on pain of his life, save the perfect knight, and with it he should achieve the Quest of the Holy Grail.

"That is all I know concerning the mystery of the

Grail," Brother Brian finished. "Mayhap the brothers at Glastonbury will have better understanding of it, for they are learned men. But I know there could be no greater quest in the world than this."

Hugh marveled at the tale, for in it the wonders of Camelot and Glaston and the Grail were one. When he had taken leave of Brian, he thought about it still, and rode slowly through the forest. He wondered how the Grail was fashioned, and how men should know it; he thought of the Red Cross knight, and of the glory that should be his. Wonder and longing filled his heart until it was nigh to bursting. He looked toward the lonely towers of Brannlyr, and thought of the weed-grown jousting field, and the ancient crumbling walls, and the weapons rusting in its keep. He was filled with anger and shame, and sudden tears stung his eyes. He wheeled his horse and dashed back to Brian's hut. As he flung himself from the saddle, Brian heard and came outside.

"Good Brother Brian, nay, I should say Sir Brian, I beg you of courtesy, let me go with you to Glaston, and if it may be, to King Arthur's court," Hugh said, and he was all but weeping in his earnestness.

At first Brian was astonished to silence. Then he asked, "Why?"

Hugh had no ready answer, but he said, "To see the wonders you told me of, and mayhap in time to win worship, for there is no glory to be won at Brannlyr; it falls to ruin."

"Yet Brannlyr was a fortress from the old Roman time, and you are its lord," Brian reminded him. "Would you forsake it because you have heard a tale of wonder?"

"I would rather be a serving man in King Arthur's hall than lord of Brannlyr," Hugh answered.

"In truth, some have come and served humbly," Brian admitted. "Sir Gareth served in the kitchen under Sir Kay the Seneschal and waited for a chance to prove his worth, nor let it be known that he was of noble lineage."

"So would I," said Hugh. But in truth he did not see himself as serving man or kitchen boy; with shield and spear and plumed crest he saw himself riding into the lists to win worship. And in his thought the shield was white, quartered in glowing red.

Brian was still thinking of Sir Gareth—how he toiled in the heat of the kitchens and bore the scorn and taunts of his inferiors, and endured all in patience until he was ready to prove his knighthood. And Brian said, "Meseems true knighthood is sooner achieved in humble service than in the lists. Foolhardiness comes of overweening ambition; for some it is harder to learn humility than to win worship. That is truth, and I learned it in the forest of Brannlyr."

But to Hugh, patience and humility and service

were pale words against the streaming plumes and banners of his imagination. "Sir Brian," he said, "I pray you, let me go with you on your journey."

"I go tomorn," Brian said, "on foot, and with a dole of bread."

"I would go too," Hugh insisted.

"Give thought to it," Brian said seriously. "The journey may be longer and harder than you think, and the end of things seldom accords with the beginning. Consider it well then, and seek counsel of one wiser than yourself. Then if your purpose hold, we may journey together."

That night when the household of Brannlyr gathered at meat, Herlewin the Chaplain sat down with them. Through the meal Hugh spoke little, for all his thought was on his talk with Brian, and on his resolve to journey with him. It seemed to him he had no need of counsel.

When the meal was nearly over Hugh said, "My lady mother, this morning I carried the alms basket to the hermit, and he bade me give you his thanks, and say the gift was over generous, and that he would share it with the poor."

"He is a worthy man, and charitable, though no true hermit," Herlewin the Chaplain said.

"Sooth, he is a knight of King Arthur's court," Hugh exclaimed. "Tomorn he journeys to Glaston, then to Camelot, and I fain would go with him. Mother, I pray you, give me leave to go to Glaston with Sir Brian."

The lady started from her place all pale and said, "My son, what childish folly is this? Think you to leave Brannlyr so lightly, you that are now its master?"

Then she bethought herself and smiled and said, "If you would go as a pilgrim to the holy place, our good Herlewin will go with you, and such men as can be spared from Brannlyr for an escort. But the matter need not be hurried, and we will speak of it another time."

But Hugh would not be put off and said, "No, Mother, I would go to Glastonbury with Sir Brian, for we have talked of the miraculous Thorn Tree, and of the Holy Grail."

At the mention of the Grail the lady grew more troubled. "Reverend sir," she said to Herlewin, "talk to Hugh and give him good counsel, for his head has been turned by this false hermit. I know that from Glaston he will to Camelot, and into the folly of tournaments and battles that may well be left to others. For mark you, it was in holding Brannlyr against the invasion of King Claudas that my lord was slain, and my father with him, and I widowed and twice bereft." And the tears of her old grief stood in her eyes.

"Lady, in that you speak truth," the old Chaplain

said gently. "No words can measure the widow's grief for her lord, nor the people's loss when their valiant leader is slain; but a people preserves the name of him who set their safety above his own, and the tale of his valor strengthens the spirits of many, so the far-off effect of it can never be measured or known. So it was when Aaron Rheged, ever lukewarm toward Arthur, delayed to bring up his forces, and the brunt of the battle fell on Brannlyr. Under your lord's command, two score men at arms held the fortress against the invaders until Gwydr brought up reinforcements and put them to flight, and Arthur's chain of defense remained unbroken. Had it not been so, the invaders would have put fire and sword to the land, and those who escaped would live by the sufferance of Claudas, compelled to pay him truage, as in the old time they paid it to Caesar. From this your lord defended them, and this they will remember. Though he was taken from them in the heat of battle, let us not call his going death, for who can die while Britain lives?"

Herlewin's words called up the old tale to the lady's remembrance, and pride in her lord filled her heart and softened her grief. And Hugh, who had not heard the full glory of it told before, sat transfixed, and his heart swelled as he tried to call up his father's face and his voice, and wished he might have stood at his side.

Then the lady raised her head and said, "I would not dull the brightness of his memory with my woman's grief. Counsel the lad as it seems best to you. Only let the custom of the castle be honored, as it was for his father."

Now the custom of the castle was this: before the young lord departed for his training in chivalry, he watched the night alone in the chapel at Brannlyr, as a seeker after knighthood kept vigil before donning his untried armor. The saying was that if the young lord was of good courage and steadfast intent, a truth would be revealed to him that would guide him on his way. Some said a voice revealed it; some, a vision. Others believed it came from within, if the youth took deep thought of himself and the task before him.

Herlewin answered, "Well bethought, my lady. It must be this night, then. At the appointed hour I will be his guide."

Hugh knelt before his lady mother and thanked her for her consent. Then he pondered Herlewin's words and wondered why the Chaplain thought to guide him, since the way to the chapel was as well known to him as the way to his own chamber.

4

The Vigil

HUGH STOOD BY the narrow window of his chamber and looked toward the cold wash of the sea. Patches of silver gilt shifted on the dark water and edged the veils of cloud that drifted across the moon. The incoming tide was running into the narrow gorge folk called the Churn, and Hugh could hear the inrushing surges break into thunder at the base of the cliff, then, hissing and seething like imprisoned dragons, fling jets of white water to the moon. He listened for each seventh wave that would thunder louder and rise higher than those before it, and he listened for Herlewin's step on the stone passageway. By the tide it was close to midnight, and he had been waiting alone for hours.

Then he heard steps on the stair, and light flickered along the wall as a torchbearer appeared followed by the Chaplain. The boy set the torch in an empty bracket and withdrew, and Herlewin stood smiling in the doorway.

"My son, it is time," he said, and motioned Hugh to follow.

His sandaled feet made no sound on the stones; his

dark robe merged into the shadows and broke into crimson folds beneath the flaring torches. The kindly old man and all the familiar scene were becoming strange and unreal to Hugh as he followed with quickening heartbeat. He saw his lady mother waiting, grave and silent, by the clustered columns that led to her apartments. She smiled and raised her hand to him, and watched him down the long passage.

Near the end, where Hugh would have turned aside to the chapel, Herlewin continued to an old stair that led down into the oldest part of Brannlyr. It was seldom used, and the single torch flickered feebly above a well of darkness. Hugh grasped the guard chain and felt his way down step by step, for his guide was swallowed up in the dark. Then Herlewin pushed open an ironbound door and they were out in the silver-gilt night, behind the curtain wall that was the castle's last position of defense. Hugh looked about, not sure whether he had ever been in that exact spot before, and he wondered why his guide had brought him there.

Ruins of massive stonework loomed about them darker than the night; free-standing arches opened to the sky; crenelated towers showed their broken crowns gilded with moonlight. This was the ancient Brannlyr, built and defended by the early lords of Alleyn. Something in the scene stirred a half-forgotten memory that Hugh could not call up clearly nor put out of mind.

The old man smiled and pointed to the opening beneath a crumbling arch. "There is the old chapel, where the custom began," he said. "It was built when Brannlyr was but a rude fort, and many have had a part in its building. The oldest wall is of clay and wattles, and part of the floor is tiled in the Roman manner. The urn once used for baptism is thought to have been brought by a Phoenician who came to trade for the white metal mined at Cornwall. The Saxon Saint Walburga stands by the altar, but some say Joseph of Arimathea was Brannlyr's first saint."

"I did not know that, nor did I know of this chapel," Hugh said. "Father Herlewin, why have we never come here?"

"When the fort became a castle with apartments for the household, a new chapel was built near them, and the old one fell to ruin," the old priest said. "But one who served your house well set it in order and tends it by permission of your lady mother, for the sake of those who have gone before. The early lords of Alleyn are buried in its crypt."

Then he moved into the arched passage and Hugh followed. As though they were expected, the chapel door opened and a dark-robed figure stood there for an instant with his face in shadow, then moved away. When Hugh and his guide entered, the chapel was empty.

Empty indeed it seemed to Hugh, bare of gilt and tapestries and bright-burning tapers. The stone floor was uneven to his feet, and flaring rushlights showed columns heavy and rudely carved.

"I leave you now, my son," Hugh heard his guide saying.

"What shall I do here, Father Herlewin?" Hugh asked, and his voice sounded small and light against the stones.

"Give thought to those who watched here before you; to those who defended Brannlyr and Britain; to those who guarded the Grail. Give thought to yourself, and pray that you may be worthy to follow them," the old man answered. He raised his hand in blessing, and when the door closed, Hugh was alone.

The dark seemed to flow toward him from deep recesses between the columns, and wavering light showed the stern eyes of painted saints watching from the walls. His step sounded loud and heavy to himself as he walked to the kneeling bench before the altar. There wax lights glowed softly on rich faded hangings and traced out squares of blue and yellow on the floor. The Roman tiles, Hugh thought, and looked to find Saint Walburga standing by. But he wanted to think of Joseph of Arimathea as Brannlyr's first saint; it gave him a feeling of kinship with the Keepers of the Grail.

And with the remembrance of Brian's tale and the

dream of Camelot, the Red Cross knight came riding into Hugh's imagination. White towers rose in the glow of the wax lights, and a shining city gathered itself out of the ancient dark. Hugh looked up to the everlasting battlements of Camelot standing against an eternal summer sky. A placid river wound through green meadows and circled a castle, and two men fished from a boat. A far-off trumpet sounded—Hugh heard it above the rising storm. And the Red Cross knight came riding, riding, and his armor was silver-bright. His hoofbeats echoed like the pounding surf, his banner streamed like a torch in the wind, and on his shield was a blood-red cross. He looked up at the shining towers and wheeled his horse, but the postern gate was an arrow flight away, across the glassy river.

The only bridge to the castle was narrow and bright and sharp as a sword. When the knight perceived it, he dismounted and took off his helm, and passed over the bridge all undismayed. Then all the trumpets sounded from the watchtowers and the people shouted together, "Open the gates to the Knight of the Grail!" The torches flashed like lightning and the glad tumult rose to thunder as the heavy door swung open.

The sound of it shook the chapel of Brannlyr; Hugh felt it tremble beneath his feet. He started as lightning played across a window and showed, in place of the shining city, a door standing open to the chancel.

Light flickered in the opening, and a bowed figure entered carrying a taper. With crouching, limping gait he moved across the chancel, then stopped to peer into the dark beyond. He raised the light, and for an instant it fell full on his face. Hugh gasped and stiffened with the old terror. It prickled through his hair and laid chill fingers along his spine, for out of the dark came the same scarred, grinning face that had haunted his childish dreams! The light swung low again and moved on, marking the halting gait of its bearer.

Hugh started to his feet, his heart pounding and his breath coming hard. The dark swirled like a tide around him, and the wax lights paled and flickered low before it. Thunder rumbled far away, and thick walls muffled the pounding surf. Hugh stood still, fighting down his fear. He must find his way to the door and open it. He took a few uncertain steps and his hand touched a wall, damp and rimed with salt. He turned again and strained his eyes into the dark.

A pale blur shaped itself to the outline of a window, and Hugh groped his way toward it. Suddenly it seemed to him that something stood in his path and barred the way. He heard a faint rustling, saw a white shape stirring, felt its touch against his shoulder. Even as he felt it, and all breathless with fear, he reached out to grapple with it. Lightly it came away in his hand and trailed to the floor—only a length of drapery stirred by a draught.

But the cold, greenish tinge of dawn, already coming through the window, showed Hugh what it had concealed. He trembled as he gazed on it, and forgot his childish fear in a new and greater wonder.

Before him stood a silken cover such as a lady might fashion for a knight's shield when it stood at rest beneath his banner in the great hall, and embroider with his device in cunning stitchery.

The cover Hugh looked upon was worked in white and silver, and its device was a cross of ruby red!

While he still gazed on it the door opened again. He heard the limping steps approaching, but now he drew nearer to the wondrous emblem and turned and waited without fear. He saw the same bowed figure, but the man's silvery hair had fallen across his scarred cheek so that his countenance was no longer terrifying, but patient and full of suffering.

He saw what Hugh had uncovered, and full silent he looked upon the device glowing blood-red in the fire of sunrise. Then he said, "Many have watched here before you, Hugh of Alleyn, but no other ever chanced to uncover the ancient treasure of Brannlyr. Verily the end of your vigil has brought you to the beginning of an adventure, and no man can foretell the end of it."

"What is the adventure, and where shall I seek it?" Hugh asked, and his voice was eager. In his thoughts all adventures ended happily, and he had forgotten

Brian's word that the end of things seldom accords with the beginning.

"That I cannot tell you," the old man answered. "Each one must find his own adventure and follow it to the end. Though you are over young, yet you are the lord of Brannlyr. Journey to Arthur's court, for there it seems adventures come to those for whom they are destined."

"I pray you, tell me your name," Hugh said, "for I have a memory of you. . . ." He stopped, for he would not, of courtesy, say more.

"I am Cormac, once a chieftain of Cornwall, and companion in arms to your noble father in his last battle when Aaron Rheged withheld his aid and let the siege fall on Brannlyr," the old man answered. "Since that day my arms have not been able to raise a weapon, and my disfigurement sets me apart from other men. By permission of your lady mother I have set in order the old chapel, and so kept the promise I made to your father—to stay near his son. Now my task is ended, and yours is beginning. Go now, and take the treasure with you. Guard it well and keep close counsel concerning it."

Hugh stepped back aghast. "It is forbidden! No man, on pain of his life, may bear the Red Cross shield," he said. "No man, except . . ." and his voice whispered away into silence.

"There is no shield beneath the cover," Cormac told him, "only a shape of base white metal. But meseems the true shield and its cover should someday come together; that may be the outcome of your adventure." He took the cover from its form and laid it in Hugh's hands.

"But noble sir, tell me how to begin!" Hugh cried. "I came to the chapel seeking a truth to guide me, and all I heard was the wind and the storm. Though for an instant I seemed to hear voices welcoming the Knight of the Grail, it may be only that I fell asleep and dreamed. And afterward I started at the thunder, and was afraid of the dark like a child, and in fear I tore away the drapery from the shield cover. Now I pray you, tell me what I must do!"

And Cormac answered only this, "Do good; right wrong; and follow the King."

5

The Journey

WHEN HUGH RETURNED to the castle he went first to his mother's apartment, bearing the silken shield cover, and when the lady saw it and heard what had befallen, she said no more against his going. But when Hugh told her that he purposed to set out on foot, with only a dole of bread, she was sore troubled; yet when she perceived his mind was set on it she agreed, asking only that he would at least depart from the castle in a manner befitting its lord. And Hugh assented, glad of her permission to go, and wishing to please her.

Thereupon she took the treasure and folded it in silk and fine linen and placed it in a leathern wallet. She bade Otho the Butler pack a dole of fresh bread and sent word to Owain, keeper of the horse, to make ready for the lord's departure. Owain gave orders to Dickon the groom, and Dickon shook Tam awake and set him to polishing the fittings of the young master's saddle.

By mid-morning all was ready, and the lady Blanche came forth and waited at the castle steps to see her son depart, and Bronwen and Moira were with her, and Herlewin the Chaplain. The news had traveled among the folk of Brannlyr, and they gathered in the courtyard and without the gates to wish their young lord Godspeed.

Hugh came and knelt before his lady mother and kissed her hand, and Herlewin gave his blessing. The lady kissed her son, and with her own hands buckled the wallet to his belt, and bade him keep it safe.

Yet she was loth to see him go, and said, "Promise me that you will return when your adventure is finished, nor leave Brannlyr long without its master."

Hugh said quickly, "I will return, Mother."

The lady smiled sadly and said, "Yet I would that I had a daughter also, to bear me company until you come again."

Then Owain and Dickon brought Hugh's horse to the mounting block and he mounted lightly and waved farewell, and rode with them over the drawbridge. When he came to where Tam was waiting, he checked his horse, and saw that Tam was holding the new fish net in his hands. And Hugh said suddenly, "Tam, I go afoot, and with but a dole of bread. Let me have the net, and I will give you . . ."

"Take it, young master, I want nothing back," Tam said eagerly. He thrust the net into Hugh's hands, and his face was redder still with pride and embarrassment.

If the villagers marveled to see their lord depart for his training in chivalry with a fish net in his hands, they cheered him all the same.

When they had passed through the market place and come to the edge of the wood, Hugh dismounted and bade farewell to his companions, and said he would go to Brian's hut afoot. But ere long he came on the hermit-knight sitting on a fallen tree among a scattering of rocks and scrub oaks. Brian showed no surprise at Hugh's coming, but rose and pointed with his staff to an opening in the trees.

"Our way lies there," he said, "to a meeting of waters beyond the hills."

The dark boughs framed a sunlit landscape that flowed in waves of gold and green down to a misty valley, then rose in a tide of rose-green and violet to the far-off slopes.

So they fared down into the valley, and journeyed through the gold of mid-morning and the white light of afternoon until they came to the far-off slopes. There they spread their cloaks and rested in the shade of a rhododendron thicket, and ate their bread with a comb of honey Brian brought. Hugh looked to the hills where blue-purple cloud shadows moved over the rose-green and violet carpet of spring, and felt the wonder of what must lie beyond.

In the long twilight they came down the last hill

to the wide water men called the Severn Sea. There were they right glad to wrap their cloaks about them and sleep for weariness. On the morrow Hugh netted them a fish, and Brian kindled a fire, and when they had eaten they set forth again.

They came upon an old man fishing from a barge, and agreed with him for passage. He grumbled because the heavy barge rode low in the swirling water, but he would not suffer Brian to help at the oars. When they came near to a reef that ran out from the opposite shore, the boatman would go no farther, but said he would land them there. He reached out and grasped a jutting rock, and Hugh marveled that he could so steady the barge, for his hand was old and gnarled as an oak root. Brian went first and Hugh followed, but he turned back for his fishing net.

The old boatman looked at him sharply and asked, "Are you still of a mind to go fishing, Hugh of Alleyn?"

Hugh started in astonishment, and looked into the old man's face. It was brown and wrinkled as a leaf of winter oak, and as the wind tossed back the grizzled hair, Hugh met the gaze of the Enchanter's mismatched eyes!

"Merlin!" Hugh's voice was only a whisper. A smile crossed the old man's face, and he bent to the oars without answering.

Now Hugh looked to the water swirling dark and

wild about him, and the narrow bridge of stones whereon he stood. Far off a gloomy tor rose like a castle above the plain, and the old man was again fishing from the barge. Hugh was perplexed by all he looked on, for it was at once strange and familiar, but he could call up no memory of it. Like one in a dream he crossed the shining bridge; then he hurried after Brian.

When he told Brian that the boatman was Merlin the Enchanter, Brian was neither troubled nor surprised, but said lightly, "The Enchanter has many disguises and appears in many places. The safety of the realm is ever in his thoughts, and he works for it in ways that are beyond the understanding of ordinary men. But see, yonder is the High Tor of Avalon, and just below it, a hill. There Joseph of Arimathea rested on his staff, and it sank into the ground and became a living tree."

"Then are we near to Glaston?" Hugh asked eagerly.

"Meseems we should come to it ere nightfall," Brian answered.

They crossed a plain where glassy streams wound among hummocks of swamp grass, and wild bitter apples grew on stunted trees. But ahead of them the way stretched fair and green, bright with springing flowers, and so they came at last to deep-meadowed Avalon. And still the dark tor frowned above them. Now Brian went ahead with his eyes fixed on the distance. Suddenly he turned and pointed with his staff.

"Look there!" he exclaimed joyfully.

Hugh saw square towers against the sky, crowned at the corners with turrets and pinnacles that soared ever higher until they seemed to touch the sun itself, and melt away in splintered gold.

"Glastonbury!" His voice choked with the wonder of it. He knew that many a quest had begun at Glastonbury, and that Arthur and his Queen had worshiped there, but he had not known that men could raise stones to such splendor.

Soon they came to a Roman road, and by that road they came, foot-weary and hungry, to the Glastonbury gate. From the gate they followed the Pilgrim Way to the porch of the Abbey church. There the wicket was closed against them, and as they considered what they should do, one came across the green and spoke to them in Latin.

"*Pax vobiscum*, peace be with you."

"And with you, Brother," Brian answered quickly.

The speaker wore a monk's habit loosely corded about his plump middle, and his face was ruddy and cheerful beneath a fringe of brown hair. Ere he spoke further, his gaze turned to the church, moving over its piers and arches, tracing patterns in the lacelike stone as though he were leafing through a well-loved book.

As if turning a page, his look moved to the roofs of the cloister, across its orchards and vineyards to the mere that stretched to the sunset. Brian and Hugh forbore to break in on his thoughts, but waited until he turned to them again.

"Meseems there can be no fairer place on earth than our house," he said.

"Fair indeed, beyond all imagining and men's power to tell of it," Brian said courteously. "We are strangers to Glaston," he went on, "come hither as pilgrims on our way to Camelot. I am called Brian, son of Rience of the Green Isle, and my companion is Hugh of Alleyn. If you are of the Brotherhood, I pray you, tell us what we should do, for it grows dark, and the way is closed."

"And we ate our last bread this morning," Hugh added.

The monk looked at Hugh and nodded in sympathy. "I am called Brother Johannes," he said. "The gate is closed against me also, and I may forfeit this evening's bread. For look you, I will go a-wandering about the mere at sunset and overstay my time, and in jest my brothers set the gate ajar for me, but too close for me to squeeze through, because I am fat. They would have me ring the Abbot's bell like a penitent."

For all that, his voice was merry and rumbled with laughter. "But come, there is bread for you, and now I see a way for me to get in, praise be."

Now the Brotherhood of Glaston had their cloister in the shadow of the church, with a house for their Abbot and a great kitchen apart, and a guest house, and many other buildings beside, all made pleasant with orchards and herb gardens and set within a wall. There was a gatehouse with three crowns above it, and that was the King's Gate; there was another gate where they distributed bread to the poor, and that was the Penniless Gate. There Brother Johannes stopped and pointed to its gatehouse, built like a porch against the wall.

"John the Almoner will be nodding within," he said. "Though it is not the hour to distribute bread, our good Abbot turns no one away. Pull the bell and Brother John will come. And if you stand so, side by side, and speak to him loudly, as you must, for he is hard of hearing, it may be that I can slip within the gate at the same time. And for that kindness I will bespeak you to our Abbot, that you are pilgrims on the way to Camelot."

They laughed with the jolly monk, and jangled the bell loudly, and all went as Brother Johannes planned.

The Almoner had no sooner returned from the kitchen than Brother Johannes came again with merriment in his look.

He said, "I told our good Abbot that two way-farers at the gate were in truth pilgrims and on their way to King Arthur's court—for meseems it must be so—and he commended me for my vigilance, and bade me offer the hospitality of our guest house, for charity's sake, and for love of the King. And I shall have my supper also."

They followed him through a covered passageway to the door of the guest house. "Here ye may rest the night," Johannes said, and called a lay brother to attend them. As they waited, he took the fishing net from Hugh's hand and tested its strength, and it pleased him well.

"A finer one I never saw," he said as he handed it back, "and I know where lurks a fish worthy of it. We have done battle, he and I, and he the winner. If you would try your luck, I can show you the place, for he stays there, I do believe, but to teach me patience and humility."

"Let us try it tomorn," Hugh said laughing. He had a great liking for Brother Johannes.

Then came the serving man, and led them to a long bare chamber with partitions running outward from the wall, making a row of narrow stalls. On the floor of each was a pallet of straw covered with a coarse clean sheet, and beside it a basin of water for washing.

"No other guests have we tonight, you may sleep where you will," the man said.

When he had brought them bread and soup thick

with vegetables and savory with herbs, they were thankful to eat and go to their beds. Hugh unbuckled his belt and placed the leather wallet close by him, and thought on his adventure in the chapel; but because of Cormac's warning to keep close counsel concerning it, he forbore to speak of it. He stretched out thankfully and closed his eyes. Peace enveloped him like a coverlet, and the silence was like far-off singing, and so he slept.

6

Glastonbury

ON THE MORROW when they had heard matins and breakfasted, the Abbot Walterius spoke with them in his writing room and inquired the reason for their sojourn at Glaston. Then Brian related the misadventure that caused him to do penance in the forest of Brannlyr, nor spared himself the blame. He told also of the happy outcome of it, and of his purpose to give thanks at the Abbey.

His answer pleased the Abbot, and he bade them welcome. He asked Hugh if he also came thither with some special intention. Hugh spoke little for shyness, but told his desire to learn of Joseph of Arimathea and the mystery of the Grail.

At that the Abbot grew thoughtful and said, "We of the Brotherhood of Glaston honor Joseph of Arimathea as our founder, but concerning the mystery of the Grail we know little. Men have told wondrous tales of it since early time, and now who can know for certain which things are true, and which are only tales of the people? Yet there is the Thorn Tree and the spring that runs red beneath it, and the circle of stones in the old

church. Brother Johannes will show them to you, for
he loves our Abbey well."

Then Brian thanked the Abbot courteously and
asked to share the work of the brothers while he dwelt
among them. So Brian went to labor with the garden-
ers, and Hugh to the great kitchen that stood in a mint
garden by the Abbot's house. The stone-ribbed roof
rose like a tower to a lantern-shaped opening that let
the smoke out and the light in. From the door Hugh
saw fireplaces in the opposite corners and two brothers
kneading bread at a wooden trough. There were store-
rooms beyond and space enough to prepare a great feast,
as they did whenever King Arthur rode to Glastonbury
with Queen Guinevere and all their courtly train.

Soon one came from the storeroom and began setting the loaves to bake, and Hugh greeted him and said
he had come to help, whereof the brother was glad, for
there was work a-plenty. Hugh fetched flour from the
stores and water from the well, and wood to keep the
fires going. He pumped the bellows until his arms
ached, and he singed the front of his hair when he
leaned too close to the fire. He watched the baking and
blistered his hands at the oven; thus he shared for the
first time the toil that produced his daily bread.

Then came Brother Johannes, saying that the Abbot had given him leave to show Hugh the places he
desired to see, even as far as the hill below the Tor.

Johannes was greatly pleased, for he loved to wander in the meadows, and fish the little streams of Glaston, and watch the sun go down across the mere. The good Abbot knew it, and sometimes gave him tasks that took him without the cloister walls. Then would Johannes overstay his time because the cuckoo sang, or small fish darted in the sunlit water. Or he would go a-fishing and, bemused by all he looked on, come back leaving his fish on the bank. So the brothers jested with him for his forgetfulness and because they loved him well.

"First we will see the old church which men call *Ecclesia Vetusta* in the Latin tongue. There, they say, was the beginning of Glaston," the good monk said.

Smallest and plainest of all the cloister buildings was the old church, built of rough-hewn stone, now weakened by time and the weather. Moss and slow-creeping lichen veined and spotted its ancient walls. Above, in niches that caught the sunlight, delicate purplish flowers sprang from wind-borne seeds, and birds nested in crannies where stones had fallen away.

Dark and bare it was inside, with naught but a simple altar at the far end. Brother Johannes stopped within the door and pointed with his staff to the floor.

"See, the circle marks the place," he said. "That is the way it was."

Hugh looked and saw a floor of reddish stone with a ring of colored stones set in lead, and twelve small golden circles around it. In the center was a single golden circle, and from it lines ran out to the other twelve.

When Hugh had looked at it awhile he said, "I pray you, Brother, tell me the meaning of it."

Brother Johannes answered, "Here did Joseph of Arimathea build his church of clay and rushes, round like a beehive, and when it had fallen away, men raised this chapel as a memorial, and caused the ring of stones to be set over the place where the first foundation stones yet lie in the earth. In the center was the altar, and the small golden circles remind us of the twelve holy ones who dwelt in little huts around their church. Now ye have seen it, and ye know."

When Hugh had looked at it a while longer, they went out together. Before them the Great Tor rose above the mere. "There is time for the hill too," Brother Johannes said. "We have leave to stay until the time for giving bread to the poor. Then Prior Tatwyn would have you help John the Almoner. Yea, there is time," he repeated, squinting at the sun. "And at the foot of the meadow is the pool where the old fish waits to plague me. If you've a mind . . ."

Hugh caught his meaning. "I'll fetch the net," he said.

They fared beyond the cloister wall into a flower-deep meadow, and it seemed to Hugh that they passed into an earlier time, into a world new-made. Soon he would climb to the place where Joseph of Arimathea had rested, and he would see the tree that sprang from his staff and lived from that far-off time to this. For it was the wonder of Glaston that the past never departed from it, but hung like a veil of shining remembrance above its cloister walls, so that those who dwelt within lived still with the ancient mysteries. Something of this Hugh felt, though he could not have put it into words; but as he walked with Brother Johannes that morning, all that belonged to Brannlyr was very far away.

So they passed through the deep meadow and skirted the mere, and came to the rise of the hill that lay before the Tor. There the lush meadow-green gave way to sparse dun-colored stubble and sun-bleached bracken that clothed the steep ascent. They bent their backs to its incline and slowed their steps and came at last to the top. There they beheld a single tree, and that was the Thorn. They looked at it without speaking, and Hugh drew nearer and stood beneath the close-laced branches and saw the thorns, and the five-fingered leaves, emerald-green against the sun. He knew the miracle of its beginning, and yet it was a tree like other trees. He wished it were winter, that he might see the marvel of its winter blossoming.

"The story of the tree ye know," Johannes said, "how Joseph rested on his staff to pray, and the staff became a living tree. Now when Joseph beheld it, he set the Grail on the ground before it as an offering, and lo, a spring gushed forth from the place, and the water of the spring was blood-red. See now, the spring."

A little away, Johannes bent over a clump of green-growing fern and lifted aside the long fronds that Hugh might look upon another wonder. In the hollow where the Grail had rested, the water bubbled red!

"Let us tarry awhile; it is good to be in this place," Brother Johannes said.

They sat down in the shade of the Thorn and Hugh looked across to the rooftops and walls of the Abbey. Was it there, or at King Arthur's Camelot, that the Quest of the Grail would begin? He picked a sprig of thorn from the ground and laid it on his knee. Idly he smoothed out the delicate leaves and turned the question over in his mind. Then he laid them flat in his wallet against the linen that folded the treasure of Brannlyr, and turned to his companion.

"Brother Johannes," he said, "where now is the Holy Grail?"

The monk roused from his contemplation and answered with a smile, "Meseems the Grail is forever with us at Glaston."

"But I heard tell—'twas Brian said it—that the Grail vanished from men's sight," Hugh said.

"Yea, from men's sight," Johannes repeated. "But

to those who dwell within the Abbey another manner of seeing is given; they see it in all time—as it was, and is this day, and as it will be—and in their memory-vision it is all one. Our Abbey does not change; though its stones may crumble and fall, its true walls stand forever, and its ancient mysteries endure. We of the Brotherhood know the Grail is forever with us at Glaston."

Then he smiled and shook his head as though he had spoken his thoughts unwittingly. "You may not take my meaning, for I cannot put it plain," he added. "But these things I think on sometimes when I go a-wandering and overstay my time, and my good brothers jest at my forgetfulness."

In truth Hugh understood it not, for his thought was on the knightly quest. So he asked, "Have you seen King Arthur's hall at Camelot?"

"Not I," said Johannes. "Ten years I had when they sent me from Cornwall to the choir at Glaston, for I was the youngest son and my mother was dead. The brothers taught me, and I grew up loving our Abbey and its way of life so I could in no wise leave it. I chose the cloister, and my father's other sons sought worship at arms."

"At Camelot, mayhap?" Hugh questioned him.

"Not at Camelot; three fought with Arthur against the Saxons at Badon Hill, and two came not back. The third rode out again when Claudas challenged Arthur's right to rule in Britain."

"How could anyone challenge the King's right, when he had proved his kingship by drawing the sword from the stone?" Hugh exclaimed. "All the knights and barons of Britain owned him king and swore him fealty."

"Not all took a willing oath," Johannes said. "Before the coming of Arthur many ambitious lords essayed to draw the sword and failed; and afterward some in their envy charged that Arthur was not Uther Pendragon's son, but a fosterling of Merlin the Enchanter."

"Nay, he is the true king!" Hugh exclaimed. "My father served him and so shall I. Leormand of Brittany says King Arthur is even greater than Caesar."

"Meseems no one could look on him and not do homage to his kingship," Johannes said. "I saw him once, when he and Queen Guinevere came hither on pilgrimage, and never saw I goodlier man nor king. But this my last brother told me when he rode hither to take leave—that Aaron Rheged, he who married with Arthur's sister, covets the throne for his son Modred, and because Modred is young, Aaron would rule in his stead. Yet he moves not openly, but spreads false rumors to the King's hurt, and delays in battle that the advantage may fall to the King's enemies."

"So he let the siege fall on Brannlyr, and my father was killed in its defense!" Hugh cried in swift anger.

"Your father left a hero's name," Johannes said gently, and Hugh looked at him in surprise.

"One who came hither as pilgrim told us of the stand at Brannlyr, and of the valor of its lord. Seven years ago it was, nay—more than that—ten," Johannes mused. "That year my last brother rode out and came not back, though he was a seasoned warrior. Now they are gone, and only a girl-child remains. She attends Queen Guinevere at Camelot because of the service her father rendered to King Arthur. He was my valiant older brother, the one most like our father." The monk's look was sad and far away, for his thoughts had gone back to another time, and Hugh was silent and waited.

"I saw her once—my niece," Johannes went on. "She was with the Queen's train when they came hither on pilgrimage. She was a fair child with blue eyes and hair like smoke, and she is named Gwynneth.

"Why, look you!" he exclaimed, and his countenance waxed cheerful. "When you are at Camelot it may be that you will see my niece. Say to her that her uncle-in-the-world thinks of her and sends her his blessing. Tell her how we climbed the hill together."

"That I will do," Hugh promised, glad that his friend was lighthearted again.

Johannes looked toward the sun. "Mayhap we should eat our bread now," he said, opening his wallet. "And since you have the net, we may as well go down by the mere."

They skirted the shallow edge of the mere and came to where the water cleared and deepened, to where an outcropping rock thrust below the surface and formed a watery cave.

"Look down," Johannes said, and he crouched on the brink and peered into the water.

Hugh looked, and saw shadows rippling brown and gold and ocher over the bottom.

"Ah, a fish for the mastery! A fish above all fishes!" Johannes whispered.

Then Hugh saw the dark shape, like a blunted arrow fallen to the bottom. The rippling light magnified his bulging eyes and the pulsing movement of snout and gills, and the lazy sweep of fin. Speckled and dark like the bottom of the mere, glinting in tarnished armor where the light shafted down on him, he seemed like some fabled creature of ancient tale, waiting to match his cunning with man or beast in underwater combat. This was Brother Johannes's fish.

Hugh took off his shoes and belt, laid his wallet by Johannes, and took up the net.

"Too swift and wily he is for that," Johannes said. "I'd thought of setting a weir for him first." He pointed to a length of net, already weighted and lashed to poles.

But before they could proceed further, a gold-green fly darted among the insects skimming the water and challenged the warrior fish. True and swift as an arrow he flashed to the surface, caught the fly, and sank to the bottom. Then, having stirred himself to action, he darted to the surface again and again—almost, it seemed to Hugh, within compass of the net. Hugh lowered himself to a scant foothold nearer the water. As he watched, there came a burnished insect with gauzy wings, and it lighted on the water. Hugh saw the fish on the bottom; knew it would rise again. In the second of its upward darting he leaned over and cleft the water with his net. Too vigorous was the stroke for that narrow foothold, and Hugh plunged into the mere.

Taken by surprise, and cumbered by his clothes and the net that he would in no wise let go of, he thrashed about and so roiled up the silt from the bottom that Brother Johannes feared he might not come up again, and was girding his robe to go in after him when Hugh got himself afloat and swam to the bank. Johannes stretched out his hands to help him, but Hugh would give him the net first; and as he drew it out of the water, a fish was in it. When the monk saw that it was dark-speckled and of goodly size, he marveled at the manner of its capture as though it were a miracle.

"Yet I repent me of his capture," he said ruefully.

"We played a kind of game, he and I, and I shall miss him on my walks about the mere."

But Hugh was glad of his prize, and set about packing it in wet fern. Meantime Johannes took up Hugh's wallet from where he had laid it, and as he glanced into the water—there was his warrior fish resting on the bottom as before!

Johannes laughed heartily and called to Hugh that it was another fish they had taken. Whereof the monk was glad, for in his heart he wished the old fish no harm, and gave over his thought of setting a weir. So they returned, laughing over their adventure, yet with a goodly prize to show for it.

A little company was already waiting outside the Penniless Gate when the fishermen returned. Hugh left his fish in fern and water by the spring, and went to help John the Almoner.

Brother John was wiry and quick in his movements, full of compassion for the sufferings of the poor, but prickly as a chestnut burr to those who sought charity undeserved. Hard of hearing he was, and he shouted his conversation as though all the world were deaf also.

He sent Hugh to fetch bread from the kitchen, and bade him stack the loaves in a great osier basket on the porch. While Hugh so busied himself, others were coming to the gate, and they waited for bread in the patient silence of the poor. When the wicket was opened, Hugh stood by the basket handing the loaves to Brother John. The Almoner knew his people, and as he gave them bread his keen gaze probed to their unspoken needs. He added a loaf to the dole of a widow with many children; he found a shirt for a man too ragged for decency; he sent to the apothecary one who limped with an unhealing sore.

As they came, Hugh watched the line and the loaves, and hoped there would be bread for all. He was seeing the poor for the first time; he saw them one and one, as they held out their hands for bread. He did not see their faces, for their shoulders were bowed with years, or with the iron collar of serfdom, or because they were humble and poor. He saw their hands, hungry and thin, or gnarled with toil, or branded on the palm with an owner's mark, and he was glad the Almoner was giving them bread. He wondered if there were as many poor at Brannlyr; he had not given thought to them. But Brian had shared his food with them, and they had called him Brother.

The Almoner was brisk and the line moved, and the pile of loaves dwindled to the bottom of the basket. Then there was but one loaf, the smallest and last of the baking. A woman's hand reached for it.

"Four children we have," she said pleadingly.

"The last of the bread today," Brother John

shouted. He was troubled because the loaf was so small. "Why did not Cerdic come himself?"

"He was hurt raising a great stone from the lord's field," she said. "If it be that his arm is broken . . ."

"Send him here—our apothecary will look to it; and come you earlier for bread tomorrow."

It was all Brother John could do, but he sighed because all was never enough.

"Wait, there is a fish!" Hugh said suddenly.

He hastened to the spring and came back with his fish. The woman was astonished at its great size, and could not believe he meant to give it to her. Then she spoke her thanks and blessed Hugh for his charity, and went away happy.

Now it chanced that Abbot Walterius came forth from his house and spoke to the woman, and she showed him the fish and told him whence it came. The Abbot looked toward the porch and saw Hugh with Brother John, and remembered him from the morning.

When Hugh left the Penniless Porch it was the hour of Evensong, and Brian came from the field. Together they went to the minster and heard the holy words, winged with music from an unseen choir, soaring above them like birds at evening.

"*Laudamus Te, Domine.* . . . We praise Thee, O Lord. . . ." The sanctuary glowed with vermilion and gold and all the jewel-fires of glass, and its clustered columns rose heavenward like prayers, offering the work of men's hands to the glory of God. When the service was ended, the monks moved in solemn procession around the church as was their custom, and ascended by a divided stair to their dorter. Still the unseen choir sang on, offering prayer and praise without end.

"*Laudamus Te . . . Laudamus Te, Domine. . . .*"

That night Brian said, "Tomorrow we set forth for Camelot."

7

Concerning the Fisher King and Other Matters

EARLY ON THE MORROW as they breakfasted, one came to say that the Abbot would speak with Hugh of Alleyn. The summons surprised Hugh, and he rose straightway and went with the messenger.

The Abbot's dwelling was spacious, stone-built with buttresses and towers and high-arched windows set with blue-white glass. It looked upon a fair garden enclosed within a wall. All this Hugh saw for the first time, for when he and Brian had been summoned to the Abbot's writing room they had entered by another way. He followed the messenger through the gate and up a stone stair to such a room as Hugh had never seen. He had seen books at Brannlyr; from them he had learned his letters and then to read. But he had never imagined a room filled with books. There were shelves of them, row on row. A few large volumes lay open on reading stands. Some, Hugh saw with surprise, were made fast to shelf or desk with a length of chain. Heavy black letters stood forth on the open pages; gold and rich color glowed in their margins. Volumes were bound in gilded leather and some in velvet—crimson, purple and blue—with silver-wrought corners and jeweled clasps. Hugh marveled that books should be deemed of such worth.

Then the Abbot entered and greeted Hugh gravely, and Hugh wondered if he had done aught to cause him displeasure.

"Hugh of Alleyn," the Abbot asked, "whence came the fish you gave the woman yesterday?"

So it was the fishing!

"My lord, I netted it in the mere," Hugh answered. "If it is forbidden to fish there I repent me of it, for I did not know."

"Methinks you were not alone in your fishing," the Abbot said.

Hugh did not answer, for he did not wish to name Johannes.

The Abbot understood, and smiled. "It is not forbidden to fish in the mere," he said, "albeit little fishing goes on there without Johannes. But this I would know —which one of you caught the fish?"

So Hugh told how he had fallen into the mere, and taken the fish unknowing, and brought it ashore when it might easily have escaped, so that Brother Johannes likened it to a near miracle.

Then the Abbot asked Hugh why he had given the fish away.

"The woman was poor, and the last loaf was the

smallest of all, and I deemed the fish large enough to feed her family," Hugh answered.

"So did the first Alleyn give fish to the hungry," the Abbot said, but he spoke as though calling it up to his own remembrance.

Hugh heard it with amazement. "The first Alleyn, my lord?"

"You have heard the tale," the Abbot said, "how, when Alleyn fished the streams of Glaston, the fish came to his net as though they would be caught. Thus he fed the hungry, and men called him the Fisher King."

"He fished at Glaston?" Hugh exclaimed. "Was he of the Brotherhood?"

Then was the Abbot astonished at the question, and asked, "Can it be that you bear the name of Alleyn and know not your lineage?"

"No one ever told me, my lord," Hugh said, but his words fell away and shame flushed his cheeks. He had never asked. The early lords of Brannlyr lay beneath their marble effigies in the ancient crypts; their devices were fading from the tattered banners in the hall, but Hugh had given no more thought to them than to the poor. Humbly he said, "I pray you, my lord, tell me who he was."

The Abbot's voice was grave, and he spoke his answer slowly. "The first Alleyn was the son of Joswe, son of Josephes, who was the son of Joseph of Arimathea. Joswe had two sons, Brons and Alleyn, and after him they were Keepers of the Grail."

When Hugh heard that he trembled and grew pale and cast his eyes to the ground, and no words came to him.

"My son, if you knew not these things why came you hither to learn of the Grail?" the Abbot asked.

"When I questioned Brian concerning King Arthur's court, he told me of the Grail, and that the quest of it would be the greatest adventure in the world. Then I besought my lady mother's leave to go with him to Glaston, and as I watched in the chapel that night methought I saw the Grail Knight pass over a bridge into a castle. . . ." Hugh's voice faltered, for he knew not where to end the tale. "It may be only that I dreamed," he said uncertainly.

The Abbot listened as though he would hear every word. "Have you more to tell, Hugh of Alleyn?" he asked. His voice was patient and his look was kind.

It came to Hugh that the mystery of his adventure was too great for him—that he should seek counsel of one wiser than himself. Who could be wiser in these things than the Abbot of Glaston? So Hugh took up his tale again, and told of the treasure of Brannlyr, and opened his wallet and spread out the shield cover before the Abbot's gaze. Then was Abbot Walterius astonished, and fell silent for a time.

He lifted a volume from the shelf and laid it on the stand by the treasure of Brannlyr. Time had crumbled the leather and flaked away the gold, but Hugh could read in dim letters on the cover:

The Book of Joseph of Arimathie

"This book telleth the adventures of Joseph of Arimathea in Britain, and is full of wonders and tales of magic such as simple folk tell their children," the Abbot said sighing. "Who now can separate the wheat from the chaff, and the false from the true? Of the Grail itself little is told, save that which you know. It maketh mention of Brons and Alleyn, and the tale hath it that the Fisher King still keeps the Grail in his castle in a land laid waste by enchantment. With the coming of the Grail Knight the Wasteland shall be freed from the spell, and the Fisher King healed of an old wound."

"Will the knight then bring the Grail back to Britain, or mayhap to Glaston?" Hugh asked.

"Are men of our own time any more worthy to dwell with the Grail?" the Abbot mused. "If a knight should achieve the Quest, and bring the Grail back among us, it would in truth be a holy relic, and a thing of great reverence, and yet . . . and yet . . ." He fell silent.

"And yet, my lord?" Hugh questioned.

"The Quest would then be over for all men," the

Abbot answered slowly. "Should not each man in his own time have a vision and a quest to follow? I wonder if the tale hath yet another meaning."

"What meaning, my lord?" Hugh asked curiously.

"Alas, I have not found it," the Abbot said. He opened the book and pointed to four lines on the fly leaf. "Methinks all we truly know of the Grail is written here."

Hugh bent over the darkened page and read:

> *Full pleyn this storye*
> *Putteth in mynde*
> *The truth of the Grayle*
> *Is hard to fynde.*

The Abbot closed the book and returned it to its place. Hugh silently folded the shield cover and laid it in his wallet.

"My son, you are of the lineage of Joseph, and a sign has been given you," the Abbot said slowly.

A thought passed through Hugh's mind like a wild bird, flown far from its proper course, that pauses with wild-beating wings and takes flight again. Hugh found no words to capture it, and looked at the Abbot in silence.

"Be not over ambitious, nor of overweening pride," the Abbot warned him gravely. "Remember, Joswe had two sons, and their sons' sons are many."

But Hugh still looked his unasked question.

"No, my child," the Abbot answered him. "The book saith, 'His name shall be called Galahad.' "

When Hugh returned to the guest house he found Brian ready to depart, and Johannes there to take leave of them both.

"You will mind your promise concerning my niece —she who is called Gwynneth, and attends the Queen," Johannes reminded him.

"With blue eyes and hair like smoke," Hugh added. "Yea, I will remember. I will tell her how we went fishing. And I leave you the net, that you may try your luck again in the mere."

When they had taken leave of Johannes they went out of the Abbey gate by the Pilgrim Way. And anon there came a clatter of hoofs and a knight on horse; with him rode a squire bearing the knight's arms and leading a third horse. When the knight saw the two afoot he set up a great halloo, and spurred his horse, and when he was come near he dismounted lightly. Hugh saw that he was young and fair of face, and the sleeves of his tunic were richly embroidered and edged with fur.

"By my life—it's Gareth!" Brian shouted, and they rushed together and made great joy of their meeting.

Thereupon the horse the squire led began to whinny and paw the ground until Brian stroked his face and talked to him, calling him Thor the Thunderer.

"Where were you taking the Thunderer?" Brian asked.

"Certes, to find you," Gareth answered. "To see that you come mounted to Camelot as befits a knight. In truth, my brother, I thought to see you barefoot and with a long beard, mayhap overgrown with moss, for they told me you had become a hermit." He looked at Brian with merriment. "Praise be, methinks there's some force in your right arm yet; you may live through another tourney."

"But how did you know? Who told you that I was in the forest—or that we should meet on the road to Camelot this day?" Brian asked.

"Merlin!" Gareth laughed. "Our old gossip Merlin —knows all and tells little that a man can make sense of. But in this matter he spoke me plain. When I recovered from the mangling I got in that last joust—my fault more than yours—he promised to send you word of it."

"That he did," Brian exclaimed. "It was the gladdest news ever I heard. This is the messenger he sent to me in the forest, Hugh of Alleyn. He goes with me to Camelot."

Gareth held out his hand. "May you find what you seek at Camelot," he said lightly, "worship at arms, or marvelous adventure, or the favor of a fair lady."

Hugh laughed and spoke his thanks and mounted behind Brian. They turned their horses toward Camelot, and Gareth spoke of many things that befell the court while Brian was away. Hugh listened for the joy of hearing him name King Arthur and Sir Launcelot and Tristram of Lyonnesse. Then they gave over talking and spurred to a swifter pace. When the sun had climbed to the zenith they stopped to rest their horses and partake of the repast that Ector the squire set for them. When Hugh saw how the squire knelt by Gareth to serve him, so Hugh felt minded to serve Brian. Then did Gareth inquire if Hugh went to Camelot as Brian's squire.

"For that he lacketh all manner of training," Brian answered slowly. "He would not know how to do on a knight's harness, nor, methinks, how to parry a page boy's swordplay."

Hugh's ears grew red with shame, and he cast his look to the ground.

"For that no blame is to him," Brian went on quickly. "His heart is so set on winning worship that he careth for little else. Verily, he declared he would rather be a serving man in King Arthur's hall than be lord of Brannlyr. So we ride to Camelot together, but what we shall do with him there I know not."

"Why, I will bespeak him to Sir Kay the Seneschal, that he may have my old place in the kitchen," Gareth laughed. "Nay, I commend it for knightly training." He held out a strong brown hand seared with an old burn. "Look you, Hugh, how turning the spit strengthens the hands; and dodging a flying pot or a buffet on the ear makes a man wonderfully agile. And if you please Lucan the Butler, you may one day become a serving man in the hall, according to your desire."

He left off speaking, and Hugh was silent with disappointment and chagrin. Were they taunting him because he lacked a squire's training—because he said he fain would be a serving man in Arthur's hall? Sooth, he had said it, but then he had spoken like a child. Was he not lord of Brannlyr? Nay, more, he was kin to Joseph of Arimathea, and he carried in his wallet a treasure they knew not of. Yet they would make of him a scullion, suffering buffets from Sir Kay and burning his hands at the spit. Swift anger flooded to his cheeks. He did not look up, but he felt Gareth's eyes upon him.

Then came the memory of how he had served in the kitchen at Glaston and burned his hands at the oven, nor minded the doing of it; for there no one was lord or scullion, but all were brothers. He seemed to hear Abbot Walterius saying, "Be not over ambitious, nor of overweening pride. . . ." Suddenly the anger left him, and he heard himself saying, "If you would bespeak me to the Seneschal, I will serve in the kitchen."

"I will speak to Lucan also," Gareth said, "for you will learn much of worship in the hall. So did I, ere Sir Launcelot made me knight."

"And you shall try your strength at casting the

bar," Brian added. "And you must tilt at the quintain until you can strike it fair and pass it unscathed. Then mayhap, one day you will ride in the lists."

Then Hugh was thankful to them, and humble in his thoughts, for he perceived they mocked him not, but sought to help him.

Anon they rode forward until they came to Salisbury Plain, and it was toward even, that is to say, vespers, for it was the season of long twilight. Before them, solitary on the plain and gray-purple against the paling sky, stood the ring of stones that was the wonder of Britain. Those who beheld it knew fear as well as wonder, and no man raised a dwelling there. Only a few sheep, straying over the downs, cropped in and out of the circle and huddled to sleep against the sun-warm stones.

But men, more fearful than sheep, believed all had been set in place by old, dark magic. They knew no men living could raise such monoliths from the ground and stand them like giants, two and two, and crown them with great mortised slabs that joined all into a massive circle. Giants, perhaps, might have done it, but not men; therefore they named it the Giants' Dance.

Others said that Merlin raised it by his craft long ago, and had a marvelous secret dwelling beneath, where erst he taught his magic to Morgan le Fay and to Nimue, who was the Lady of the Lake. Nimue learned white magic, but she was affrighted of black magic, and fled from Merlin back to her lake. But Morgan le Fay learned it all.

And Nimue was ever friend to King Arthur, and told him much to his help; but Morgan le Fay sought ever to do him harm, and that was pity, for she was half-sister to the King. So men said in the olden time.

In that ancient circle the travelers tethered their horses and partook their evening meal. Afterward they sat apart, speaking little, watching the shadows creep over the Avebury hills and flood the plain, conquering all save the giant stones, for the moon rose in a greening light and cast over them the color of old magic. It was not like the morning-magic Hugh had felt in the meadows of Glaston; it was older and wilder, and Hugh thought of the sunless chasm where he had first seen Merlin, and of the wild gray water they had crossed in his barge. As he lay on the ground thinking these things, his ear caught a muffled beat. Gareth heard it too and started up. Brian listened and said, "There are two of them."

They mounted lightly and readied themselves, and they stayed watchful in the shadows of the stones. Then Gareth rode forward and took cover in a thicket, and there kept watch of the road.

Anon they heard the hoofbeats come nearer, and pass, and die away on the road to Camelot.

Then Gareth came back and said, "This much I saw: a bay horse and the rider muffled; and this I saw plain: his shield was half green, half argent."

"Aaron Rheged!" Brian exclaimed.

"And Modred," Gareth added. "Rheged thinks the time is ripe." His voice was grim, and he held out his hand. "Arthur is king!" he said fiercely.

"Arthur is king!" Brian clasped Gareth's hand in his own. Together they looked at Hugh. Quickly he placed his hand on theirs and repeated, "Arthur is king!"

Gareth touched him on the shoulder. "Hugh of Alleyn," he said, "you are neither squire nor knight, yet you are stouthearted, and you are already lord of Brannlyr. On you, more than on either of us, may depend the peace and safety of Britain. For Brian, after his father, will be lord of the Green Isle, and I with my brothers will hold the Orkneys. But Arthur's enemies are not on our northern islands, they stand around his throne. If they should gather strength to rise against him, would Brannlyr stand for Arthur as it did in your father's time?"

Hugh would fain have cried out "Brannlyr for Arthur!" but he mistook Gareth's meaning. He thought of the weed-grown jousting field, and the fading battle flags, and the unmended walls; in his ignorance he wondered if Brannlyr would prove worthy to withstand another siege. Shame covered his cheeks and held him silent.

"Where lies your allegiance, Hugh?" Gareth cried. "When you come to the age of knighthood will you promise to right wrong and follow the King, or will you some day be won over by the wiles of Morgan le Fay, and the persuasions of Rheged and Modred?"

"Never that!" Hugh cried, and there was a touch of anger in his voice. "I shall always follow Arthur! I promise it now—I promise to do good, to right wrong, and to follow the King."

"Well said! I'd no need to ask, since you'd spoken already," Gareth said, good-humored again. " 'Twas the sight of those two that put me off my aim. They ride to Camelot, and we must not be far behind."

"We shall be on the road by sunup," Brian said, and after that they slept.

On the morrow they journeyed through a green gloom of over-arching trees into fields of hyacinth and small petaled flowers like suns that maids called the day's eyes. It seemed to Hugh that the air grew suddenly still and crystal clear. He lifted his face to its coolness, and lo, he saw the shining towers of Camelot where erst he had seen nothing but meadow and blue sky!

8

Camelot

A MONTH OF DAYS AND NIGHTS, of sun and rain, had passed over the world of men since Hugh crossed the bridge into shining Camelot, but beneath its dreaming towers the days flowed in light from sunrise to starshine to sunrise again, as though all time were a single day. The air was ever fresh and crystalline, cool from the touch of far-off snows, fragrant with roses that drifted their petals over the garden walls.

Ladies walked among the flowers, dreaming the days away, listening for the clatter of hoofs in the courtyard that would tell of the end of a quest and a knight come home. Pages tuned their lutes and whiled away the waiting with songs of love and death and summertime, while fountains spun them rainbows in the gardens of Camelot.

In the low-vaulted castle kitchens the air was breathless with heat from the fires that were never allowed to go out, heavy with smoke and burning grease, loud with the din of iron pots and brazen voices. There Hugh toiled among the scullions who turned the spits and stirred the stews and basted the roasts that were carried in endless procession to the hungry knights of the Round Table. If Hugh had grown somewhat thinner, he had grown taller and stronger, and his hands were toughened and scarred as Gareth's had been. He had learned to take a buffet and hold his tongue, and to work for his daily bread.

Though Hugh was a very scullion in the castle kitchen, out in the river-meadow he knew himself to be a knight of Alleyn. For there the youths who aspired to knighthood gathered to practice tilting with the blunted spears and dented shields provided for their training, and they rode the straight narrow courses between barricades as they hoped some day to ride in the sanded lists.

Thanks to Dickon, the groom at Brannlyr, and Dickon's Tam, Hugh could manage a horse as well as any; but when they came to tilt at the quintain, he took his fair share of punishment. The quintain was a stout pole set in the ground with a cross arm at the top. A battered shield was fast to one end of the arm; a swinging weight hung from the other. The would-be knight charged past it, aiming his blow at the shield. If he missed the center the arm spun around, and the flying weight smacked him hard. He learned to ride low, head down, to aim straight, and to take his buffets without whimpering.

These thundering, bruising, wind-swept hours were what Hugh lived for; he felt a wild joy in the dizzy running away of the earth beneath his horse's hoofs, in the brazen shout of spear against shield, in the feeling of being strong and free and almost a knight. And when an adversary proved stronger and sent him hurtling to the ground, he was proud to remount and contend with him again, without anger or excuse.

Sometimes the knights watched their practice, sitting their horses proud and aloof. Sometimes Brian came, and Gareth, but Hugh saw them seldom. His companions now were the young squires. Among them were Ector, and Sir Tristram's Dinadan, who had already been promised knighthood, and Gryflet, a lighthearted squire who served King Arthur.

Sometimes a strange youth stood on the fringes of their tumult, watching with down-lashed furtive glance and thin, curled smile, holding himself apart and his thoughts in silence. An uneasy, secret pride sat on him. Whether he had skill surpassing theirs, or whether he feared to contend with them, the others never knew, but a luckless youth who suffered a blow or a fall felt the sting of his wordless mockery. It was Gryflet who told them the watcher was Sir Modred, the King's nephew, lately come to court. Whether he had in truth been knighted, or whether he was so called of courtesy, because of his kinship to the King, Gryflet did not know.

Then Hugh remembered the night riders on the

road to Camelot, and the oath of allegiance to Arthur, sworn in the dark circle of Stonehenge. Hugh did not reveal it, but he felt his anger rising against Modred, because he was Aaron Rheged's son; yet he was the King's nephew as well. Thereafter Hugh sought to avoid Modred in all ways he might. But there came a day when they chanced to meet, and this was the manner of their meeting.

Modred had been idling about the tourney field when the youths gave over their practice, and as Hugh walked toward the castle courtyard he saw Modred ahead of him. They were both approaching a part of the wall that swept out in a semicircle below a corner tower. Hugh supposed the wall enclosed a garden, because vines tangled along the top and spikes of blossoms waved above it; but the gate was always shut, and Hugh had never seen inside. He saw Modred pause uncertainly by the gate. As Hugh came near, a gilded ball flew over the wall and fell like a small sun on the grass. At once he heard a childish shriek, and as Modred picked up the ball a porter swung the gate open. A fair-haired girl appeared; she was about ten, with a dimpled, laughing face, and a broken toy in her hand. It was a carved and gilded cup atop a wooden handle, and from it hung the raveled string that had held the golden ball.

"My cup-ball flew away," she began. "Did you

see . . . ?" She caught sight of it in Modred's hand. "Oh, yes, that's it." But as she came forward to take it, he put it behind him.

"Not yet," he said, teasing her. "What is your name?"

"Vivien," she answered.

Modred tossed the ball in the air and caught it while Vivien watched anxiously. "Do you know the lady Gwynneth?" he asked.

At Modred's question Hugh stopped, and waited for the child's answer.

Vivien looked back to the gate where the old porter was waiting, and she nodded vaguely. "Please give me the ball, sir," she said, holding out her hand. "We are not allowed outside alone, and he may not keep the gate open."

"First find the lady Gwynneth and bid her come to the gate. Say the King's nephew would speak with her," Modred commanded.

"I attend the lady Gwynneth, but I do not bid her," the girl said stubbornly. She was biting her lip and she looked near to tears.

Modred shrugged, tossed the ball and caught it, and hid it behind him while Vivien watched helplessly.

It was shame to him, Hugh thought, to tease a child so. He stepped forward quickly, twitched the ball from Modred's fingers, and tossed it lightly over the wall. Vivien darted after it, and Modred turned on him swiftly.

"You dared approach the King's nephew unbidden!" he exclaimed angrily. "A kitchen scullion who thinks to be a knight!"

But Hugh was looking past the furious Modred to where a young girl was coming down the rose-bordered path. Her hair curled like a puff of smoke beneath a cap of netted gold, and her eyes were as blue as her gown. By these things Hugh knew her name, even before he heard Vivien calling, "I am here, Lady Gwynneth!"

Modred saw her also, but Hugh recklessly brushed him aside and gained the gate first.

"Lady Gwynneth, I pray you . . ." She looked at him in surprise, and Hugh of courtesy dropped to his knee. "I pray you, give me leave to speak. . . ."

"Hear him, lady, for he is a knight full courteous," Vivien broke in. With a scornful look at Modred she added, "The other is but a churl, and no true knight."

A dimple showed in Gwynneth's cheek, but she stifled her laughter in grave courtesy. "Rise then, sir knight, and speak."

Hugh answered, "Lady, I am called Hugh of Alleyn. I bring you greeting from your kinsman, Brother Johannes of Glastonbury."

Surprise showed in Gwynneth's face and she said

eagerly, "Dear to me is my kinsman Johannes. His messenger is welcome."

Modred still stood by watching and listening, and his anger grew that he was unnoticed and that Hugh was preferred before him, and he said full scornfully, "I marvel that a lady should hold converse with a kitchen boy."

The blue eyes looked on him coldly. Gwynneth turned away and with a gesture invited Hugh to follow. The porter closed the gate behind them. Gwynneth led him to a marble bench by a fountain, and when she had seated herself Hugh sat on the grass before her as she bade him.

"Tell me how Johannes fares," she said at once. "Is he in health?"

"Of that I am certain, lady," Hugh answered, "and to me he seemed the happiest of men. And the best," he added, as if to himself.

His answer pleased Gwynneth. "Pray give me all his message—I would you could remember his words."

"I do remember, lady," Hugh said. "These were his words: 'Say to her that her uncle-in-the-world thinks of her and sends her his blessing.' "

She smiled, but Hugh saw the quick tears. He added, "He bade me tell you how we climbed the Tor together."

"I pray you, tell me that also," she said.

So Hugh told of his sojourn at Glaston, and of the goodness of Brother Johannes, and of his old fish in the mere.

"I remember the mere," Gwynneth said suddenly. "I had forgotten it, but I remember now! Once when I was little, the Queen took me to Glaston with her train. We were there three days, the King and Queen and all their company. When I grew weary of the long ceremony and the feasting, Brother Johannes would take me walking in the meadow, and once we sailed on the mere in a little boat. He was always merry and kind, and I wept to part from him."

She added thoughtfully, "If Johannes were not of the Brotherhood of Glaston, mayhap he would dwell in my father's hall; for my father came not back from the war with Claudas, nor left a son to hold his lands. If Johannes were there, I might see Cornwall again."

"Is Cornwall fairer than Camelot?" Hugh asked in surprise.

"I did not mean that," Gwynneth said quickly. "Surely there can be no fairer place than King Arthur's Camelot. But sometimes I have a kind of memory of the sea, and long black cliffs running down to it, and a salt-cold rush of wind. . . ."

"It is like that at Brannlyr!" Hugh exclaimed. "The storm-tide rushes into a gorge below the castle and dashes spray into the air like white dragons flying. Even in summer the water feels like cold knives. Moira says the old water-gods still dwell there, but I have never seen anything but seals."

"In truth Brannlyr must be like Cornwall; I would hear more," she said, smiling.

Suddenly in his mind's eye Hugh saw it anew—the battle-proud towers that watched landward and seaward; the battle-scarred walls that held off the armies of Claudas as they held off the sea. So he pictured Brannlyr to Gwynneth with pride in his voice, and she listened with a far-off look as though she were seeing it with him. He went on to tell of the siege of Brannlyr as Herlewin had told it in the hall.

"A noble tale—and a proud fortress!" she exclaimed. "How many brothers have you to hold it in your honored father's place?"

"No brothers, lady," Hugh answered. "My lady mother is at Brannlyr with Moira and Bronwen, and Herlewin. . . ."

"But she has your father's knights to defend it," Gwynneth said.

Hugh was silent. How could he tell her that the knights had long since departed, and only the village folk remained to defend the fortress, and with no chieftain to command them?

She did not wait for him to say it. "Some day, if the quintain spares your head, you will go back to be lord of Brannlyr," she said.

"Some day . . . I will go back," he said, and in his heart there was a sudden longing for the sea.

"Sometimes I think a wall of shining air shuts us away from the other world," Gwynneth said slowly.

"The other world?" Hugh said surprised.

"The world as it is at Brannlyr, and at Cornwall," she said. "As I think it must be everywhere save here at Camelot. In Camelot the air is clear as crystal, or a mist drifts over it like a dream. Marvelous adventures befall the knights of Camelot, and wonders that would be beyond belief in Cornwall. Sometimes I think Camelot is not a place at all, but a memory of a far-off time."

Hugh looked across the shaded lawns where ladies walked in trailing silks and jeweled slippers beyond the rainbow mist. Fragile and dreamlike it was in truth, beside his memory of rugged Brannlyr. He remembered that Merlin had raised many-towered Camelot for the King.

A lady and a knight were walking in converse with each other beneath an avenue of trees. The knight was in armor with a crimson cloak cast back from his shoulder. The lady was fair as moonlight, regal and grave of demeanor.

Gwynneth said, "It is the Queen and Sir Launce-lot."

So at last Hugh looked on the great Sir Launcelot, though at a distance, and marked his noble bearing and his proud dark face. "He is in truth the noblest knight in the world!" he exclaimed.

"He is the flower of all chivalry and the Queen's Champion," Gwynneth added. "He is come to take leave of her, for the King is sending him to settle a dispute between the lords of Albany and Cornwall." Her look grew troubled. "Modred must have known, and for that he lingered by the gate," she said. "His mother, the King's sister, warned me that Morgan le Fay sets him to spy on the Queen and Sir Launcelot. He was angry that I did not bid him enter, for no knight may enter the ladies' pleasaunce unbidden."

"Brother Johannes told me that Aaron Rheged covets the throne for Modred," Hugh said. "Now that I have seen Modred I marvel that a man could foster such a wan hope, even for his own son."

"Aaron knows he cannot accomplish it while Arthur lives. Now he would have Arthur name Modred his heir, but the King is not persuaded." She bent and picked a flower from the grass. "I fear Modred," she said.

"Surely you need not fear him, Lady Gwynneth," Hugh said quickly. "Never have I seen noble youth so craven in spirit. He loiters about the tourney field like a shy damosel, and takes no part in knightly exercise. Never have I seen him make essay at arms, either on horse or afoot."

"He does not fight with a knight's weapons," Gwynneth said, "but with false rumors devised by Morgan le Fay—that Arthur is not in truth King Uther's son, and that Sir Launcelot casts great love to the Queen. . . ."

"Why, there are not three people of greater worship in the world!" Hugh exclaimed. "I would make that good with my life."

Thereupon Gwynneth looked up and smiled.

"Some day I may make trial of Modred's prowess," Hugh said, and the thought pleased him mightily.

But later as he walked back to the castle kitchen he thought no more of Modred, but that he had seen Sir Launcelot, and that Gwynneth's eyes were very blue, and that she looked not at all like Gillian, the dairymaid at Brannlyr, who was the only other damosel Hugh could call to mind.

9

At the Feast of Pentecost

IT WAS KING ARTHUR'S CUSTOM to hold high court every year on the feast of Pentecost, for that was the anniversary of the founding of the Round Table. Therefore, when the time drew near, he sent messengers and trumpeters throughout the realm to summon all his knights to Camelot. Their trumpets rang over the chalky sea-cliffs and broke the stillness of the ancient forests, and echoed through every hamlet and town. The knights heard and gave up their questing, and sped over the stone-bright roads to Camelot. Launcelot rode from Albany with his brother Bors; Bedivere, the King's Cupbearer, set out from the border of Wales, and Sir Tristram, with Dinadan his squire, hastened from the court of his uncle, Mark of Cornwall.

Kay the Seneschal was making great preparation for the feast, and no one could tell of all the baking and roasting and boiling that went on in the kitchen, nor describe the marvelous sweetmeats that were made for the King's table. Red-faced scullions fetched and carried and turned the spits, polished the silver, and ducked the buffets of their masters whose tempers grew ever shorter. Hugh toiled with them and his lot was no better than theirs, save that he still hoped for some far-off high adventure.

On the day of the feast, Lucan the Butler strode into the kitchen and shouted above the din to Kay the Seneschal.

"I must have another lad in the hall, and none of your heavy-footed churls, either. I want a lad that's tall and well-favored with all his wits about him, and one that won't fall over his own feet."

His sharp eyes passed over the toiling scullions until they fell on Hugh. "You, there!" He beckoned, and Hugh came.

"Your name?" the Butler demanded.

"Hugh of Alleyn."

"Whence came you?"

"From Brannlyr, in the marches of South Wales," Hugh answered.

Lucan seemed well satisfied, and without waiting for Kay's assent, he took Hugh out of the kitchen. So it was that Hugh came at last to Arthur's hall and saw the great Round Table spread for the King's feast, and the knights' proud names above their devices on the chairs, and the mysterious Siege Perilous veiled in white samite so that no man might look on it. Dishes of gold and silver were set for each place, save that before the Siege Perilous. Platters heaped with dates and figs and all manner of confections and fruits stood ready on the sideboard, and by them was a covered golden basin that held perfumed water for washing. Hugh was high-hearted when Lucan told him he was to serve in the hall, but his hands trembled when he lifted the golden basin at Lucan's order.

Then Lucan instructed him in the ceremony of hand-washing, how he should hold the upper half of the basin in his left hand and the lower half in his right and, kneeling before the King and Queen, uncover the perfumed water. When they held their hands over the empty basin, then should Hugh pour the water over them, nor spill a drop on the lady's gown. When they had dried their fingers on the towel he would carry on his arm, then must he rise and, bowing his head before them, return the two golden halves to Lucan.

Again and again they rehearsed it, until Lucan was satisfied that Hugh could perform it with grace befitting the Queen's service. Then he sent Hugh to be fitted with a silken tunic and shoes edged with the gray fur men called vair. On the sleeve of the tunic were three small crowns in gold stitchery to show he was the King's servant. So he came proudly back to the hall, still wearing his leathern wallet, for he would not be persuaded to leave it off.

Then Sir Bedivere the Cupbearer came with his golden pitcher and stood by his brother Lucan. After him came servants with flowers and sweet-smelling herbs to strew on the floor. After a time certain of the knights began to come in and go to their places. By their names and devices Hugh marked them: tall dark Tristram of Lyonnesse; Percivale the good knight; Palomides the Saracen; and the King's nephew Gawain, and his two brothers, Gaheris and Gareth—the same who befriended Hugh—and Brian was with them. Two other nephews of the King were there also—dark-hearted Agravaine and the young Modred, favorite of Morgan le Fay. But Launcelot's place was still empty, and it was next to the Siege Perilous.

"Launcelot hath been long away from court," Lucan said.

"Yea, he tarried in Albany lest Magdelant should return and harry the border again. But of surety he will be here tonight, for we met by the way and rode some miles together toward Camelot," Bedivere said. Then he told how a damosel overtook them and prayed Launcelot to go with her—for why she would not tell—saying only that he might do her behest and still come to Camelot for the feast.

Then Hugh saw that all the places were filled save those two. Voices fell lower and ceased; the hush of waiting came over the hall. At a sudden flourish of trumpets the doors swung wide; light glinted on jewels and cloth of gold; the knights rose in homage to Arthur and his Queen.

Hugh took the golden basin in his hands and stood

by Lucan and Bedivere until Lucan whispered, "Now!"

Then Hugh was kneeling before his sovereigns, tilting the golden shell until the perfumed water spilled gently over two pairs of hands—one strong and brown, the other pale and long-fingered, with an emerald set in twisted gold.

When the ceremony was finished Hugh could not forbear to raise his eyes. He looked on the King's countenance and saw there such courage and high resolve as marked him for the truest knight in the world. After the courtly train had passed, Hugh's eyes held the image of Guinevere, lily-fair and golden, with a veil over her shining hair and eyes like blue-green water. He watched as the King and Queen mounted the dais to the high table. He heard the long sweep of blade against scabbard as the knights unsheathed their swords. On their sword hilts the fellowship swore anew the oath Merlin required of them when he laid on the Round Table the Order of Chivalry:

> I will never do a cruel or unjust deed, nor fight in an unjust quarrel.
> I will give mercy to those that ask it, and help to all ladies and damosels in distress.
> I will fly from treason and all untruthfulness.
> I will ever strive to do good, right wrong, and follow the King.

When the ringing voices ceased Taliessin swept the harp and Bedivere filled the King's cup and thus the feasting began. One thing only was lacking; those who knew the King remembered that he wished never to begin this high feast without witnessing some marvel.

But to Hugh, standing quietly in attendance as Lucan bade him, all he looked on was a marvel. The hall was bright with banners and jewels and rich attire, warm with laughter and good fellowship. Taliessin's harp threaded the merriment with highhearted song, and Dagonet the fool crouched like a many-colored ball by the King's chair. Then Hugh saw that only one place remained empty at the Round Table; Sir Launcelot was sitting, dark and thoughtful, in his place by the Siege Perilous.

At that instant Gryflet, the King's squire, came in haste as though he had been running, and broke in on Dagonet's tale.

"My lord King, I come to tell you of a marvel!" he cried, all breathless.

"Now our feast lacks nothing!" the King exclaimed. "Say on, Gryflet, and let all hear!"

"My lords," Gryflet said, "this is the marvel I saw, and Ector and Dinadan with me, in the field where we tilt for practice. We saw a block of stone, red like marble, and stuck into it was a fair rich sword. There were precious stones in the pommel and curious letters wrought in gold about it. But the greatest marvel is this: the stone, together with the sword, floats just above the river!"

Above the murmurs of surprise Hugh heard the King saying, "I will see this marvel!"

But then came Dinadan, breathless as Gryflet had been. Dinadan said, "My lord Arthur, more have I to tell you of this thing! After Gryflet departed, we watched the stone, and it hovered nearer and nearer, and at last it held itself still above the water. Then Ector and I spelled out the letters on the sword, and this is what was written:

> *No man shall draw me hence, but the one by whose side I ought to hang, and he shall be the best knight in the world.*

All those who heard looked to Sir Launcelot. The King marked it and spoke for them: "Sir Launcelot, the sword ought to be yours, for of all knights you have most fame, and I deem you the best knight in the world."

Launcelot answered him gravely, "Of a truth, my lord, the sword is not mine, nor have I the hardiness to put my hand to it. One greater than I shall draw it."

While he was still speaking there came an old man leading a young knight into the hall. The ancient figure was robed in white and a hood concealed his face so that no one knew him. On his arm he carried a rich cloak furred with ermine.

The knight was clad in red armor, save that his head was uncovered. An empty scabbard hung by his side, and he carried neither sword nor shield. So fair of face and figure was he, so noble yet modest in demeanor, that the company fell silent, waiting to hear his name.

"Peace be with you, fair lords," the old man said, and passed by them to stand before the King. "Sir," said he, "I bring you a young knight worthy to sit at your table; he comes of a king's lineage and he is kin to Joseph of Arimathea. By him marvels shall be achieved in Britain."

Hugh, hearing it, grew pale and trembled. The name had not been spoken, but he knew. He knew it was for this moment he had left Brannlyr. His dream in the chapel, the treasure he carried at his side, the ancient mysteries of Glaston, all seemed centered to this event, to the coming of the youth in red armor. What meaning it had for him he could not tell, but certain he was that his own adventure was drawing near.

He heard the King saying, "Sir, you are right welcome, and the young knight with you."

Then the old man bade the knight do off his armor, and over his coat of red sendal he cast the cloak furred with ermine. Then he said, "Sir knight, follow me."

He led the knight to the place beside Sir Launcelot, and the whole company fell silent when he laid his hand on the Siege Perilous. They watched as he drew away the silken cover and let it slip to the floor; they read in letters of gold the name: *Galahad*.

"Sir knight," said the ancient one, "this place is yours."

The knight inclined his head courteously and seated himself in the Siege Perilous, while many marveled that one so young and untried dared to sit in that place. Launcelot turned to the youth and made him welcome, and as they talked together, some said the young knight resembled Sir Launcelot.

The new-made knights who served at table quickly bethought them to set a place before the stranger, and speedily they served him all manner of dishes to his liking. So the feasting went on; Taliessin made music and Dagonet tumbled and jested, but the merriment was not as before. Wonder took the place of mirth, and those who had been quick to take up a challenge or follow a quest sat restive and pondered the meaning of what had befallen.

When the feast was over the King and Queen left the high table, and the knights rose in their places. When the King came to where Galahad was standing by Launcelot, Launcelot said, "My lord, this is my son Galahad. His mother was Elaine, daughter of King Pelles, who comes of Joseph of Arimathea's line. He was nourished in an abbey and taught by Nacien the hermit; he has learned also the customs of knighthood. As I rode thither from Albany, a damosel came from King Pelles, and at her behest I rode with her to the abbey.

There I gave my son the high honor of knighthood this very morn."

"In that you did well," the King said, "for now the fellowship of the Round Table is complete. With the coming of this knight the great Quest draws nearer."

Launcelot and Galahad went with the King, and the knights followed after, and all the company went down to the river meadow to see the wonder of the floating stone. Kay and Lucan and Bedivere went also, and Hugh went with them. In his eagerness he would have sped straight to the water's edge, but he checked himself and followed after, as befitted a servant. He slipped into a screen of willow and swamp alder that led to the river. Many a time he had gone through it like a cat, but he bethought him of his furred shoes and silken tunic and came out again. Now the company was well ahead and he hurried after, the last to reach the place.

The magic color of twilight flooded field and river, and the square red stone hung like a dark ruby just above the water. From it the sword rose in a streak of light. The company, seeing it, fell silent. The Queen shivered and drew back, and Gwynneth came bringing her cloak. She cast it lightly over the Queen's shoulders and stood beside her. Only the King approached the stone and read the golden letters. Then he turned to the assembled knights. He looked first to Sir Launcelot, but

Launcelot had said the sword was not for him. Yet the King would have a proven knight make trial first, and he turned to Sir Gawain.

"Fair nephew, essay to draw the sword," he said.

Gawain answered, "Sir, save your good grace, I may not put my hand to it, for I wit well I am not the best knight in the world."

"Then essay it at my commandment," the King said.

"At your commandment, my lord," Gawain answered courteously.

Gawain grasped the hilt and pulled, but the sword did not move. Then he put both hands to it, and pulled mightily, but he could not draw it, nor move it a whit. Still the King would make trial again, and he thanked Gawain and turned to Sir Percivale.

"Percivale, not without cause men call you the good knight," Arthur said. "At my commandment, try to draw the sword."

Percivale put forth all his strength, and though he was a mighty warrior, he had no better fortune than Gawain. Then King Arthur looked to his newest knight.

"Sir Galahad, two right good knights have essayed and failed," he said.

"My lord, that is no marvel," Galahad answered, "for this adventure is not theirs, but mine. If the King wills, I will make trial."

The King gave assent, and Galahad put his hand to the sword and drew it lightly out of the stone. A murmur of wonder rose from the hardy knights who knew the strength of Percivale and Gawain; then in awe-struck silence they watched the stone sink quietly beneath the water. Galahad stood smiling before the King, and the King knew, and all those present, that in the world of men there was none his equal.

"My lord, for surety of this sword I brought no other," Galahad said. "Here by my side hangs the scabbard to it."

The King said, "In truth the sword is yours, Sir Galahad. May God send you a shield also."

So Galahad sheathed the sword and ended the adventure, and the company went their separate ways. Hugh walked alone, not without a shadow of fear at the wonder of it all, but filled with eagerness too, for he knew that the adventure of Joseph's shield and the treasure of Brannlyr was surely beginning, as Cormac had foretold. Truly, as Gwynneth said, the wonders that befell in Camelot were past belief.

10

Two Tournaments

THE NEXT DAY Hugh and his companions were in the field casting the bar when Gryflet came in haste to tell them that the King had proclaimed a tournament. The youths gave over their game and crowded around Gryflet to hear more.

Gryflet said, "After the adventure of the stone, the King thought to hold a tournament that Sir Galahad might prove himself before the knights of the Round Table. The knights approved it, and they agreed to remain at court until after the jousts, all save Sir Agravaine.

"When I brought word of it to the Queen, she was well pleased, and bade me say she would order splendid preparation to be made, and all her ladies promised to attend in their richest apparel. And as I was returning, the Queen's messenger overtook me to say she would offer a fair jewel as a prize for the knight who should be judged of most prowess in the lists."

Then Hugh, who had longed to see a tournament above all else, cried out, "When will it be, Gryflet?"

Gryflet answered, "The heralds are already on the roads. It will be three days hence."

As the Queen's preparations went forward, all the court declared this would be the most splendid tournament held in many a year. It was noised about that the prize was to be a ruby of great size, set among others in a golden circlet. Some, who knew the story of the jewel, told it with many head-shakings and talk of ill omen. Others laughed and said, "Who would not risk all for such a prize?"

The story of the jewel was this: On a bleak day, November-cold, Launcelot and Bors and Bedivere journeyed homeward together from the northern marches of Wales. As the chill sun struck the height of a sea-cliff it seemed to them that a tongue of flame writhed from the skeleton arm of a bleached tree. Bors did off his armor and made his way up the cliff with great peril and gained the tree. He found the flame to be a circlet of rubies hanging from a deserted eagle nest. When Bors brought it down the great ruby flashed with such unearthly fire that it seemed to him not a natural stone, but an evil eye. So great was the loathing he felt for it that he would have cast it into the sea. But the others said it was of great worth, and the circlet richly wrought in gold, and at length they took it away with them and gave it to the Queen. An old goldsmith, who saw the stone, begged the Queen to cast it away. "No true ruby, that; an evil fire burns at its heart. I felt it grow hot in my hand," the old man said.

Some called it an old man's fancy, but the goldsmith looked on the splendid preparations and said, "It will be the last tournament."

On the morning of the tournament Hugh was at the field soon after sunup. Pennons whipped in the breeze above row on row of striped tents which would be furnished with meat and drink for the knights' refreshment. The lists were being freshly sanded, and armorers were setting up their forges nearby in case of need. In and out of the tents went squires and grooms, busy with armor and harness. Hugh thought that Dinadan would soon be arming Sir Tristram, and Gryflet would sit his horse beside King Arthur; but Hugh was squire to no one.

The King's place was marked by a glittering standard bearing the red dragon of the Britons surmounted by three golden crowns. Pavilions on both sides of the lists were hung with silk and tapestries; the Queen's place was shaded by a canopy of ruby-red velvet crowned with branches of the green yew, which was the Queen's own tree.

In that pavilion Hugh saw a tower of cushions approaching, and they bade him good morning in a childish voice. Then the cushions toppled, and some fell over the rail, and Hugh saw the face of little Lady Vivien.

He laughed and helped her pick them up, saying, "It seemeth me, Vivien, you are ever a damosel in distress."

Then Gwynneth came, and reproved Vivien for her heedlessness, though she was laughing. She greeted Hugh courteously, and he her again. Gwynneth's dress was rose-color with ribbons of silvery blue, and the hem of it curved like a rose petal on the grass. As she passed into the Queen's pavilion, Hugh followed with his arms full of cushions. He set them down and cast about in his mind for something to say. Gwynneth stood smiling at him, and a rosy flush mantled her cheeks. Hugh thought it strange that a damosel should be so like a flower.

Gwynneth looked at the pavilions cushioned and draped with cloth of gold, then across to the field of rainbow-colored tents, and she said, "Surely no tournament ever equaled the splendor of this!"

"That may well be," Hugh agreed, "though I have never seen a tournament. Above all things I have wished to see Sir Launcelot in the lists—or Sir Tristram."

"Certain it is that you will have your wish," Gwynneth smiled. "Surely they will contend, and many other good knights besides, for all the Round Table will be in the field at the King's behest."

"All save Agravaine," Hugh amended.

She looked at him, surprised. "Why say you so?" she asked.

"Gryflet said Agravaine has departed the court," Hugh answered. "He went the morning after Pentecost."

"And Modred?" Gwynneth asked quickly. "Did Modred go with him?"

"No, we have seen him about the tourney field and in the hall," Hugh answered. It seemed to him the lady Gwynneth thought overmuch on Modred.

As though she divined his thinking, Gwynneth said slowly, "If I should tell you a thing that befell at Pentecost . . ." She paused as though she wanted Hugh to speak, and all the laughter was gone from her face.

Hugh said, "If you should tell me, lady, I would not reveal it."

She nodded, as though his answer had been what she waited for, and she said, "During the feast I waited outside the banquet hall with the ladies who attend the Queen. As the company came forth to see the adventure of the stone, I thought to fetch the Queen's cloak, for the air was chill. So I hastened to her chamber and found the cloak, and came out by another way which was nearer the river. As I ran across the grass of the ladies' pleasaunce, I saw a lady in black hastening to the gate before me. So she came first to the porter's lodge and pulled the bell rope. But it was not Giles the porter who came at her summons; it was Aaron Rheged!"

Gwynneth paused, and Hugh said quickly, "I pray you, say on, Lady Gwynneth."

She glanced back toward Vivien, who was still arranging cushions to her fancy, and then continued. "I moved back among the orange trees by the wall, and I watched Aaron open the gate. It was Agravaine who entered. They went down a shadowy path together, and the lady with them. Then I knew her for Morgan le Fay!"

"An ill company!" Hugh exclaimed. "What chanced after that?"

She shivered. "I will tell you what chanced, and I would it had not!

"I saw that Aaron had left the gate a little ajar, and I thought to slip out unnoticed. But just outside I came face to face with Modred, who was about to enter. I turned swiftly and pulled the door shut, and I heard the iron bar fall into place. So cunningly wrought it is, that it cannot be raised from the outside. Wit you well, Modred's face was full of anger! For a moment he barred my way. I held out my arm with the gold cloak, and he knew it for the Queen's, and let me pass. But they will not forget I saw them!

"I take no thought for myself," she added quickly, "but for my lady the Queen; for when I told her, she . . ."

Gwynneth's voice faltered away. Hugh followed her look and saw Modred standing just below the rail of the pavilion.

"Pray go on, Gwynneth, what did the Queen say?" Modred asked mockingly.

"Eavesdropper!" Hugh vaulted the rail to face Modred.

Modred shrugged and glanced away. "What is it to the King's nephew if the Queen's spy chooses to gossip with a scullion?" he asked insolently.

When Hugh heard the double insult he was wroth out of measure. He did off his jacket and shouted, "Defend yourself!" He clenched his fists and braced for battle.

"Fool! Would you raise your hand against one of Arthur's blood?" Modred's face was dark with fury.

"He is right, Hugh! You cannot!" Gwynneth cried. "Leave be!"

Hugh straightened and moved close to Modred. "Yea, that were unseemly," he agreed. "But hark you, Modred, the King himself does not scorn to joust with his knights, though he is above them in degree. Unless you be craven—and I may not believe otherwise—get on a horse and risk a fall with me!"

Modred had the look of one led into a trap. Before he found an answer, he heard Gwynneth laugh quietly, and her scorn made him reckless. He strode to the tent where the squires' weapons were kept, and returned with breastplate and shield and blunted lance. He called a groom to bring him a horse.

Hugh likewise armed him, and came back to the pavilion and said, "Lady, I engage me to do battle with yonder knight—if knight he be—for the discourtesy he uttered in your presence."

Gwynneth smiled and said, "Gramercy, fair knight. I am beholden to you for your courtesy." She took the silver-blue ribbon from her hair and held it out to Hugh. "In token thereof I offer this ribbon as my favor, if it please you to wear it in the lists."

Hugh took the ribbon and thanked her in courtly fashion, and bound it to his shield arm.

Then came Vivien, bearing a tasseled cushion. She held it out to Modred, saying, "And I offer you this cushion, Sir Modred, to ease the fall."

Modred rode scowling away from their laughter to the range end and shouted, "Leave be this child's play!"

Hugh rode lightly to the opposite end and wheeled his horse. They dressed their shields and couched their lances, and Modred shouted, "Have at you!" So they rushed together at a great wallop.

As Hugh bore down on Modred he braced himself and readied his lance and aimed to the center of Modred's shield. In the instant before they came together, it seemed to Hugh that Modred leaned away from him in the saddle, as though he shrank from the blow. Speedily Modred pulled himself back, but Hugh perceived he had not command of his weapon. Hugh dropped his own lance, therfore, and his shield parried the glancing blow Modred dealt him. Hugh galloped past, and he was laughing when he turned his horse at the range end.

"Craven! Did you fear to trade blows with me?" Modred shouted.

"Never will I strike a knight who has the disadvantage," Hugh answered. "If you can sit your horse without flinching, have at you again!"

Then Hugh spurred his courser as hard as he might, and so did Modred, and they rushed at each other like charging boars. Hugh readied his lance, glad for those bruising hours of practice, and again aimed for the center boss of Modred's shield. His aim was straight and his arm did not fail him, and the force of the blow drove Modred backward over his horse. His feet flew from the stirrups and he hurtled over his horse's tail and sprawled on the ground. For all his clumsiness, Modred was still the King's nephew, and Hugh held back his laughter. He checked his horse and leaped down to help Modred rise.

"You were fairly overcome, Sir Modred," he said. "Therefore I charge you to ask the lady's pardon for your discourtesy."

But Modred strode away speechless, white-faced with anger, except that blood trickled from his nose.

Gwynneth looked at Hugh and smiled, but her eyes were troubled.

"We all take our falls," Hugh said lightly. "He is not hurt."

"No, but I fear others will be." Gwynneth shivered. "Modred casts a shadow on Camelot."

But the shout that came from the armorer's tent was loud and gleeful. "Well done, Sir Hugh!" It was Gryflet, and he had seen it all.

When the sun had dried the dew from the grass, it climbed the sky until it overtopped the highest towers of Camelot, then hung above them like a golden shield on a field of azure. From four entrances to the lists came four silk-clad heralds, and they mounted by spiraling stairs to four small balconies and blew their shining trumpets to the north and the south, to the east and to the west.

And Hugh, perched high in the branches of an ancient oak that overhung the jousting place, looked across the long slopes of the fields and saw the sun splintering from a forest of spear points and glancing

from a hundred shields. Banners and plumes, jeweled harness and saddlecloths made a slow-moving river of color. At its head rode King Arthur with a company of kings—King Carados of Scotland and King Anguish of Ireland, King Uriens of Gore and King Clarence of Northumberland.

Hugh did not know their names, but by the richness of their trappings he knew they could not be less than kings. With them were the knights of the Round

Table, and Launcelot and Tristram rode at their head.

When at last the procession drew near, down came the heralds from their balconies, and they stood four-square in the center of the field and blew their trumpets while kings and knights rode in at the gates and spread over the field like a tide.

When the King was seated by the royal standard, knights and kings rode by companies to the lists, and some went to the scaffolds set up for the judging and some to the pavilions. The heralds mounted their balconies again and turned toward the castle and sounded their trumpets. At the first note the portcullis was raised and the draw lowered, and the Queen's procession appeared.

First came a company of young knights in white armor with plain white shields. Never in any battle or tournament did they carry their own coats of arms, for they were the Queen's knights. Then came twin pages in green, on milk-white palfreys. One bore the Queen's banner on which was embroidered the green yew tree; the other carried the ruby prize on a silken cushion. Then Queen Guinevere, in gold and white and green rode between two of her knights, and after them came knights and ladies, two and two. The procession circled the field, and the ladies filled the Queen's pavilion like many-colored flowers while the knights rode on to the lists.

The heralds sounded their trumpets again and proclaimed the opening of the tournament in the name of the King. The first jousting was to be among the young knights—the White Knights against other new knights still untried in battle.

Hugh climbed lower and set himself astride a stout bough and looked down through a fork onto the field. From there he thought to learn something of how the knights handled their weapons, to watch the thrust that would unseat a warrior, the parry that would turn it aside. But when the signal came, a swirling tide of men and horses charged into the field in a tumult of thundering hoofs and clashing weapons and ancient battle cries. Hugh's ears rang with the din and his eyes could scarcely catch the swiftly changing scenes. Knights were being unhorsed all over the field, and Hugh never really saw it happen. If he glimpsed two knights in combat, he quickly lost sight of them in the press of men and horses, and a second later two others were contending in that place.

But he was highhearted just to be there, and soon excitement shut his ears to the din and sharpened his eyes. He began to recognize knights and horses, and sometimes to follow the weapon play. He saw Brian in the press of the Queen's knights; he saw the lightning thrust called foining; he cheered Brian through the oak leaves when the White Knight went down.

Those who were unhorsed early in the joust retired from the field, and those who remained doubled their efforts, especially the White Knights; for one who did well that day might be chosen to sit at the Round Table next year at Pentecost. It was King Arthur's custom, if he lost a knight in battle, to choose one of the Queen's knights to take his place. So the White Knights fought valiantly, like men well-proved in battle. King Arthur's young knights did no less, but fought knee-to-knee with them, and they gave them blow for blow.

Another young knight charged into the fray on a white horse. He carried a shining lance and a jeweled sword, but all who saw him marveled that he bore no shield. Hugh knew him by his red armor, and by the sword he had drawn from the stone.

Hugh eased out on the bough as far as he could, and set himself to watch the white horse as eagerly as he had watched the Thunderer. He gripped the bough with his knees and felt the white steed galloping beneath him; he parried each thrust with Galahad, and together they dealt many a blow as Galahad struck down the White Knights that rode at him one after the other. When those unhorsed retired from the field, many passing good knights remained, and Galahad contended with them, often hand-to-hand. If a spear shattered they dismounted and rushed together on foot, and Sir Galahad took many a stout blow. But his helm was so hard that no sword might cleave it; no sword could prevail against his, and he fought with the strength of ten.

While Galahad was so engaged, Brian led a company of Arthur's knights against the Queen's. Brian's men fought in close formation and held together against all comers. No company of the Queen's men could prevail against them; they pulled down White Knights on the right hand and the left. In that manner Brian and Galahad won acclaim before the King and the Round

Table, and Hugh was glad that it was so, for he loved those two knights above all others. When the heralds gave the account of those unhorsed, the honor lay between Galahad and Brian.

Those who had watched from the pavilions were also divided—some declared for Brian and some for Galahad—and they would see the two contend together for the victory. Galahad and Brian were willing, and when they had rested awhile, they rode into the lists against each other.

They clashed together so fiercely that their spears shivered in pieces; their horses reared and pawed the air. They dismounted lightly and whipped out their swords. Out of courtesy Brian cast away his shield, and they rushed together afoot.

Then indeed was Hugh's heart divided, for he was loth to see either overcome. Never before had he seen such masterly sword play. The lightning thrust, the instant parry, the nimble footwork and the unflagging zeal of both knights showed they were indeed well matched. Because they were young and strong, masters of their weapons and of themselves, they contended for more than an hour. Those who watched from the pavilions marveled that either could endure so many strokes. Shouts of "Galahad! Brian!" mingled with the ringing of steel.

At length Galahad dealt Brian such a buffet that it

jolted him to his knees, for Brian had begun to weary.

And Brian said, "I yield me! Sir Galahad, hold your hand!"

Therefore Galahad sheathed his sword and took off his helmet and held out his hand to Brian.

Brian rose and took off his helm also, and said loudly that all might hear, "Sir Galahad, certain I am that I never knew a man of your might, save Sir Launcelot of the Lake."

And Galahad answered before all the people, "Sir Brian, you also are an able fighting man."

The trumpets rang out and the judges proclaimed the honor to Galahad, since he dealt the winning stroke. Then Galahad went and knelt before Queen Guinevere, for he served no other lady. The lovely Blanchfleur, Sir Percivale's lady, crowned him with a chaplet of the Queen's yew, while roses rained around him, cast by the Queen's youngest damosels.

Then Queen Guinevere bade him rise, and said courteously, "Sir Galahad, in truth you have quitted yourself most worshipfully, and I deem you worthy to contend for the ruby prize."

Galahad made courteous answer: "From that joust I beg you will hold me excused, my lady, for to me the Queen's yew is above rubies. Since I have had a full share of honor this day, I beg leave to depart."

His answer pleased the Queen, and she gave him leave.

"By my head," said Sir Launcelot from his place by the King, "he is a noble knight and a mighty man."

When the heralds proclaimed the Ruby Joust, a great medley of men and horses overspread the field. Many noble knights were in King Arthur's party—too many to name all—but among them were Sir Gawain and his brother Gareth, Sir Bors and his brother Lionel. Palomides the Saracen was with them, and Tristram of Lyonnesse, and Sir Lavaine who served Sir Launcelot. But Launcelot kept his place by King Arthur, for he would not contend in the field lest he diminish his son's honor.

In the other party were the King of Northgalis and Carados of Scotland; King Anguish of Ireland and the King of Northumberland; and Galleron of Galway with the King of a Hundred Knights. At the sound of trumpets both sides rushed to the attack, with a great hewing down of knights and kings. Sir Gawain unhorsed King Anguish, and Gawain was overthrown in turn by Northgalis. Lavaine rode to Gawain's aid and got him on horse again, while Bors and Palomides held off Northgalis and Carados. Gareth spurred into the press and smote down on the right hand and the left. Tristram thrust in mightily and pulled down Galleron and

Northumberland and slashed off their helms. Then the knights of those kings rode against Sir Tristram, and he smote down thirty of them before his spear shattered and Dinadan brought him another. With that spear Tristram laid on more furiously than before, so that some who had been eager to contend with him now sought to engage themselves with other knights. King Carados rode at a great wallop against Palomides and dealt him such a buffet that the stroke troubled his brains and set him reeling in the saddle. Swiftly Tristram came to his aid, and thrust down Carados with a stroke.

Carados said, "Who is this knight who doeth such marvelous feats on King Arthur's side?"

They told him: "Sir Tristram of Lyonnesse."

"Woe is me that ever I met him, for by him I have been overcome," said Carados.

All those who were watching freely gave the honor to Sir Tristram. So likewise did the judges, and the heralds who gave the count of those unhorsed. Then the King bade the heralds let cry an end to the tournament, and the Queen's prize was awarded to Tristram of Lyonnesse. Straightway he begged the King's leave to depart, and so rode toward Cornwall, bearing the ruby to the beautiful Isolde.

Then Hugh climbed down from the oak tree, bedazed with the splendor and the tumult of his first tournament, and he made his way back to the hall.

11

The Vision and the Quest

AFTER THE TOURNAMENT the knights of the Round Table assembled to feast in the hall and the King sat in their midst, but the Queen dined apart with her ladies. A hundred and fifty knights save two—Agravaine and Tristram—sat down at that table together. The hall was brave with the flags of chivalry, and the royal standard glittered behind the King's chair. Each knight's banner was unfurled above his place and his shield hung on the wall beneath it. Only the space of the Siege Perilous was empty, but all who witnessed the jousting knew that in all the company there was no knight more valiant than Galahad.

Lucan the Butler set Hugh to helping the young knights who served, and while those at table talked of high adventure and quests to be achieved on the roads they would take tomorn, Hugh listened and counted himself fortunate to be even a serving boy in Arthur's hall; yet he wished he might change places with Ector, who served Galahad and Launcelot.

As the meal was nearing its end and Hugh was

waiting attentively at his station, the daylight paled and the sun cast a rosy light into the hall.

"It betokens a fair day for our departure," Sir Gawain said.

Even as he spoke the door opened and a damosel entered, all in white. She went to King Arthur and greeted him courteously and asked a boon of him.

"Say on, what is your behest?" the King asked.

She answered, "Sir King, my lady Nimue, who is called the Lady of the Lake, is come hither, and she prays the King's leave to enter. But she bids me tell you this: if you receive her and that treasure which has been entrusted to her keeping, it will be the beginning of the greatest adventure that may ever be in the world, and the cause of great dole and sorrow to the realm. Sir King, my lady Nimue bids you choose."

All who heard it were greatly astonished, and each thought to himself how he would answer, if he were king.

King Arthur said, "I marvel greatly at this saying, for it seemeth me that a great adventure should not bring dole and sorrow to a realm that has so many hardy knights eager to win worship. But to forego the greatest adventure in the world—that would in truth be cause for sorrow to many a knight, and one for which men in the aftertime would call us craven. For a man ought not to think first of his own safety or happiness, but whether he acts in a good cause or a bad one. If this be truly the greatest adventure in the world, then surely it must be for a good end."

To that all the knights assented heartily, and they praised the King's wisdom.

Then King Arthur said, "Bid the lady Nimue enter."

The doors opened again and the Lady of the Lake rode in on a white palfrey. She was clad in white and gold, and carried a shield on her left arm. She dismounted and bowed low before the King. All the company watched as she crossed the hall and stood by a carved pillar; and she took the shield and hung it on the pillar.

She said, "On pain of death, let no man take down this shield but the one who by right ought to bear it."

When the knights heard it they were astonished to silence, but Hugh looked on the shield and trembled. He clutched the leathern wallet at his side, and heard his own heart drumming in his ears. He could not take his eyes from Nimue's shield, for it was white, and marked with a blood-red cross!

When Nimue departed the rose light faded, and the hall grew dark as before a gathering storm. In the half-dark another lady entered clad in somber black, and she came midway into the hall before anyone was aware of her. Then, as the sun breaks through a rift in the storm clouds, so a beam of light from a high window passed through the darkened hall and rested on the shield. Galahad rose and went to the pillar and took down the shield, and he stood with it in the light. When the lady beheld it she uttered a loud shriek and covered her face and fled. Those who saw her close knew her for Morgan le Fay.

Then a great wind arose and blew the doors and windows shut, and a clap of thunder shook the hall. The beam of light widened to a shining shaft that fell full on the shield of Galahad. The knights beheld it and started

up in wonder. Within the shaft of light a form gathered, took shape in glowing red and moved, a light within the light, above the Round Table. To some it was but the red glow of sunset; to some it had the form of a chalice covered with red samite; but Galahad looked on it and cried, "It is the Holy Grail!"

Each one who heard tried to apprehend the image, to fix it in sight and memory that ever after he might tell it among men: "I was there when the vision appeared to King Arthur's knights; I too saw the Holy Grail."

But only to Galahad was it fully revealed; the vision was his as the shield was his. As he named the Grail its form dissolved into the light around it, and that too paled into the common twilight of the world. Then Galahad took the shield and hung it on the wall by the Siege Perilous.

But Modred bowed his face in his hands and wept.

Then Gawain, the King's nephew, said, "My lord Arthur, of a certainty it was the Grail, as our brother Galahad hath said, though veiled and hidden from our sight. Surely now the great adventure is beginning. Meseems there can be no greater quest than this—to follow the roads of the world in search of the Holy Grail. Therefore, my lord, I pray you give me leave to follow in the high adventure which Merlin promised when he laid upon us the Order of Chivalry."

Gawain's words fired others with the same resolve. and in that hour many knights pledged themselves to follow the Quest of the Grail. First among them was Galahad, whose quest it was from the beginning; and Percivale, who was called the good knight, was with them also; and Launcelot, the Queen's Champion, with his brothers Ector and Lionel. There were many others also, but Brian and Gareth were not with them.

When King Arthur heard their vows he admonished them, "What you have sworn, that you must perform."

But his heart was heavy as he released them from his service and gave them leave to ride forth on the morrow. Hugh knew he must ride with them, though they were the mightiest of the Round Table. They would know by the treasure he carried that the Quest was for him also. He trembled in his haste to unbuckle his wallet; he spread out the embroidered shield cover and bore it to the Siege Perilous. The beating of his heart made his voice strange to his own ears as he knelt and offered his treasure.

"Sir Galahad, I bring you the treasure of Brannlyr, which belonged to the knights of Alleyn, for now I wit well it ought of right to be yours. And I beg leave to ride with you and serve you as your squire, for I too am of the kin of Joseph of Arimathea." So Hugh spoke in full courteous and knightly fashion, and he was proud to offer his gift and tell his lineage. But of the Grail he said nothing.

Those who sat by were astonished, but Galahad received the gift graciously and fitted it to his shield. Then he bade Hugh rise and took his hand and said, "Kindred we are, Hugh of Alleyn, the eighth generation of two brothers. Yet like a faithful squire you took thought to furnish my shield with a cover before we ride forth tomorn."

Hugh, hearing it, understood that he was chosen. Though he could scarce speak for the joy of it he said, "Sir Galahad, I promise to serve you faithfully with life and limb, as you command me."

Galahad answered, "Those who follow the Quest go not as knight and squire or master and man, but each will ride as fortune takes him, for each man's way is his and not another's."

Then Hugh was downcast and entreated him, "Sir, if I may not do you service, then let me follow, even if only at a distance."

Galahad smiled and answered, "Nay, we shall set out as brothers, though for us the same road shall have two endings."

On the morrow the knights heard mass together at the minster, and the King with them, and Hugh attended Sir Galahad. Afterward they gathered for the last time about the Round Table, and for the last time

Hugh served them, not in a servant's livery, but in the woolen tunic he had worn from Brannlyr. He was ready and eager for the time of riding out, impatient as the horses pawing the stone-bright courtyard. When the meal was over, the knights were armed in shining greaves and breastplates, in plumed helmets and golden spurs.

Queen Guinevere came into the courtyard with her fairest ladies, and Blanchfleur and Gwynneth stood by the Queen. The King said farewell to his greatest knights, and his heart was heavy as he wished them Godspeed. Launcelot knelt before the King and Queen, and Arthur said, "Lever would I forfeit half my lands than see you depart this realm, Sir Launcelot."

There were tears in the Queen's eyes as her Champion departed, and sad was the leavetaking of many another knight and lady.

Hugh was thinking how he might say farewell to Gwynneth when the child Vivien caught his sleeve and said, "Sir Hugh, my lady Gwynneth bids you Godspeed." Of her own accord she added, "I wit well she is loth to see you depart."

Hugh remembered how he and Gwynneth had talked of Glastonbury and Brother Johannes; the dried sprig of thorn still lay in his wallet—he had seen it when he gave his treasure to Galahad. Now he was minded to give it to Gwynneth. He lifted it out and a silver-blue ribbon clung to the stem.

"That was Gwynneth's ribbon!" Vivien cried, well pleased. "I shall tell her you carry her token on the Quest."

Hugh quickly put the ribbon out of sight and held out the twig to Vivien. He was embarrassed and somewhat mixed in his speech. He said, "Pray give this to the lady Gwynneth and tell her it is from the Holy Thorn at Glaston. Bid her keep it and think of me, as she thinks of her kinsman, Brother Johannes." Before he could amend the speech more to his liking, Vivien darted away laughing.

Hugh sought out Brian and Gareth, for they were not with the departing knights, and Hugh wondered greatly at it. He remembered Brian's eager words in the forest of Brannlyr: "the Quest of the Holy Grail will be the greatest adventure that any knight may have in the world." Already the time was at hand; why was Brian not with them?

The two knights were glad to see him and wished him Godspeed. Suddenly Hugh was loth to leave Brian. He thought of all the knight's kindness to him, and he tried to speak his thanks.

Brian laughed and said, "You have repaid all by your worshipful conduct in the lists. Since Gryflet spread the word that you walloped Modred backward over his horse's tail, many a knight would be proud to confer on you the Order of Chivalry."

"Yea, we are loth to see you go, Hugh, for we hoped to have you for our squire, or even that you might take us for yours, that mayhap we might have the pleasure of seeing you do it again," Gareth added.

Sir Gawain sat his horse nearby, and the King came to him and said, "Ah, Gawain, Gawain, now in truth shall dole and sorrow fall upon this realm, for the noble fellowship of the Round Table is broken forever. The flower of our chivalry rides forth today, the heroes who drove the invader Claudas from our shores and kept the King's peace in the realm and righted the wrongs of the oppressed. Heavyhearted I am at this parting, fair nephew."

Gawain bowed his head, for he knew his hasty speech had spurred many to the Quest.

When Hugh heard the King's words the shining light of the morning paled; he saw Modred alone, watching. Suddenly he knew why Brian and Gareth remained with the King. He remembered the hand-fast oath sworn in the dark circle of the Giants' Dance, because Modred and Aaron Rheged were riding to Camelot. Gareth had asked him, "Where is your loyalty?" and he had promised to follow the King.

"Brian, how can the King rule without his knights?

Why does he not forbid their going?" Hugh besought him.

"The King has said, 'What ye have sworn, that ye must perform,'" Brian said gravely. "That is a knight's duty."

Then Hugh was sorely troubled, for of certainty he had sworn fealty to Arthur, though the King did not know it. The King had released those who vowed to follow the Grail, but Hugh was not in truth one of them. His only vow was to follow the King, and no one knew how the matter lay but himself. "What ye have sworn, that ye must perform"; must he then give up the shining Quest that would never come again in the world, and the fellowship of its chosen knight? He might have put the question to Brian, but already there was a stir in the courtyard and the knights were mounting. Galahad's white horse was being led forward. Hugh said farewell and hastened to help him mount. Then he looked back to where the King stood surrounded by the remnant of his faithful knights. With all his heart Hugh wanted to stand with them. But Galahad was waiting.

"Up, brother!" Galahad said smiling. "The time is now!"

The groom was standing by with a horse for him, and Hugh's eyes blurred when he saw it was Brian's Thunderer. As he mounted, the Queen's youngest damosels came with their arms filled with flowers and scattered them in the pathway of the knights. Vivien tossed a handful of roses at Hugh and wished him Godspeed. A blossom caught on his sleeve. He thrust it into his cap, and Vivien was well pleased.

Hugh looked back for the last time. Gwynneth still stood by the sorrowful Queen, but she met Hugh's look and raised her hand and smiled farewell. Now the knights were pressing forward. There was no time to ask Brian another question, no space to turn the Thunderer. Uncertain and troubled, Hugh was swept across the drawbridge with the tide of men and horses. So the knights rode out of many-towered Camelot to the adventure of the Grail.

12

Wherein a Wrong Is Righted

THE KNIGHTS HAD SAID THEIR FAREWELLS in the hall, and only for a little time did the company ride together. Every man took the way that pleased him, and at each crossroad, at each forest path, someone turned his mount and took up his quest alone, until only Hugh and Galahad rode together.

They rode through midsummer fields dappled in gold and green, where the earth-men pruned their orchards and tended bees and herded sheep like drifted snow on the hills. The breeze carried the smell of new-turned earth and ripening fruit and new-cut grass. Thor flung back his head and flared his nostrils to the clover smell and whinnied his animal joy. Hugh breathed deep and shouted with him, whereat Galahad laughed, and they let their horses go at a great gallop as they willed. Hugh marked how Thor's hoofs thundered over the ground, and felt his great strength beneath him, and saw his mane whipping the wind like a banner, and he loved the horse and had pride in him.

As they journeyed, the men of the land knew them for King Arthur's knights and gladly offered them bread and honey in the comb and early-ripened fruit. "While King Arthur's knights ride abroad we till our lands in peace," they said.

Three days Hugh and Galahad rode through the green land of Britain and slept in hedgerows and open fields, and they talked of many things. Hugh told of his home at Brannlyr, and of things he had seen at Glaston. Concerning Glaston Galahad asked many questions. Joy lighted his face whenever he spoke of the Grail. When Hugh asked where they should seek it, Galahad told him they must ride where fortune led them and take what adventures befell them; they must traverse the dreary Wasteland and come at last to the Castle of Carbonek. There the Lame King—some called him the Fisher King—waited to be healed by the coming of the Grail Knight. There, in some mysterious way, the Quest would be achieved. Hugh wondered how it should come about, for Galahad said nothing of tourneys or battles or winning worship at arms.

Beyond the farmlands they passed through a deep wood of oak and beech where a serf tended swine, and he told them of a hermitage where they might seek shelter. The good man received them kindly, and when Galahad told him they followed the Grail he rejoiced and gladly offered them food and lodging. On the morrow as they departed, he foretold that they should meet

Nacien, the holy hermit who would counsel them; and Galahad was glad, for it was Nacien who had instructed him in the abbey where he was reared. Anon they took up their journey and left the green and forest land, and came to bare stony ground and earth mounds left by men of old time. Galahad pointed to an ancient earthwork that lay like rings within giant rings on a distant slope.

"There the men of the north stood fast and held to their land when the Romans thought to be masters of all Britain," he said.

As my father and Cormac held Brannlyr against Claudas, Hugh thought. He looked back toward the long road from shining Camelot to the barren ground they stood on. All of it was Arthur's Britain. The unanswered question rose to trouble him again. How can the King hold it without his greatest knights? How can he keep peace in far places without the Round Table? But he did not speak of it to Galahad.

From that place chance led them westward. As they came to the sea-girt cliffs, fog blew in around them and swirled into the crevasses and hid the track, so that in the narrow passes they could but trust to their horses. Hugh gave the Thunderer his head and patted his mane and encouraged him. Thor shook his head and whinnied obedience, and went, wise and sure-footed, through the fog-shrouded way. So at length they descended to a flat rock shelter, and glad they were to rest the night.

Hugh lay and listened to the moaning of the surf and thought of the crags of Brannlyr, and how the flood tide swelled steel-bright beneath the moon. He had missed the sea in Camelot, as he had missed the smell of new-turned earth and the cool touch of rain. He fell asleep trying to remember how things were in Camelot. It unrolled like a dream tapestry of ladies in trailing silks and knights in shining armor; all he saw clearly was King Arthur standing forth with his remnant of faithful knights, and Gwynneth waving farewell. The rest was, as Gwynneth had said, like the memory of a far-off time.

Hugh slept but little. He awakened in the gray-green morning and thought himself back at Brannlyr. He felt a sudden longing to plunge into the steel-cold sea, to battle against it as he and Tam had done many a time. He climbed down over the rocks to a gravelly shingle, did off his tunic, and plunged in. He had forgotten the shock and force of the cold. It knocked the breath out of him and caused him to struggle mightily. When he came ashore and shook the water from his eyes, he saw the fog had thinned, and there was a tower a little way off, and beyond it, a castle. Therefore Hugh hastened that way to request food and hospitality for

Sir Galahad, for that was a squire's duty. Now it chanced he saw a damosel within the gate and he inquired who was lord of the castle and the tower.

"No lord, sir," she said, "but a lady keeps this tower. And the castle, which is of right hers, was taken away unjustly, and another lady holds it with many men-at-arms, and boasts that her champion, Pridam le Noire, is the greatest knight in the world."

"Now there are two wrongs!" Hugh exclaimed. "The wrong done your lady, and the boast of the lady in the castle. For the greatest knights in the world are these four—Sir Launcelot, the Queen's Champion, and his kinsman Sir Bors, Tristram of Lyonnesse and Sir Galahad, the high prince."

"Since you name Sir Launcelot, I know you speak of King Arthur's knights," the damosel said. "I would that one of the four might chance this way, for great fame have they for righting wrongs."

Hugh answered, "It may hap that one will come this way sooner than you think." And he hastened back to Galahad.

When he had told the tale Galahad said, "Let us see what can be essayed to amend this wrong."

When they were come to the tower an old porter was keeping the gate and he would not open to them. But when Galahad told him they were of King Arthur's court he seemed glad, and hastened within. He came again speedily and opened the gate, and led them to a well-furnished hall. Then came the same damosel, and courteously helped Galahad do off his armor. She offered them water for washing, and sat them down to meat and drink. The lady of the tower, a fair young gentlewoman, welcomed them and sat at the table and talked with them courteously.

When the meal was nearly over in came a squire, and he said, "Madam, I am come from the lady of the castle, and this is her word: 'You must provide yourself with a champion tomorn, for I will have this tower and its lands unless you can find a knight who will prevail in your behalf against Pridam le Noire.'"

Then the lady sorrowed to tears and said, "Alas, that I should be disinherited of the last that is mine!"

Galahad said, "Be of good cheer, lady, for we are come hither to right a wrong. Tell me, who is this Pridam le Noire, and how stands the quarrel between you?"

The lady answered, "Pridam le Noire is a recreant knight greatly feared in these parts, and I will tell you the cause of the quarrel.

"My father left me the castle and this tower and all the lands thereto, and knights and servants enow. Now there was a rich baron called Anaiuse, who cast great love to this lady long ago, and to win her favor he gave her of his lands and authority over many of his knights, and always she sought more, and added it to her own, and thereby became very rich. Then Anaiuse died, and the lady gained more of what was his. Now she is old, and greedy beyond measure, and she has taken Pridam le Noire as her champion. She makes war on me continually, and has slain many of my knights and taken my castle and driven away most of my people. Now she would have even this tower, the last of what was mine."

Galahad was wroth to hear of such greed, and he said, "In truth, this quarrel is in God's cause as well as yours. Send word that you have found a knight who will do battle with Pridam le Noire."

That night Hugh and Galahad were well lodged in the tower, and in the morn the lady came and saluted them, and they went with her to the chapel and heard service. Galahad would not break his fast until he had done battle, so Hugh helped him arm, and served him in all ways as a squire. So they rode together to the field with such knights as the lady could still command. There they saw Pridam le Noire.

Pridam was fearful to look upon, mounted on a black charger and armed in black, even to the plume in his helmet. The lady of the castle waited in a little pavilion nearby.

When the lady of the tower came into the field she went to the other and said, "Madam, you have done me much wrong, yet I am loth there should be this strife between us."

"You may not choose," the old lady said. "Let the contest begin."

Then the heralds announced the names of the knights and the cause of the combat, and declared that whichever knight had the victory, his lady should possess all the land and the fealty of those who dwelt on it.

Then the knights rode apart, each to his own side. At the signal they rushed together like charging boars and their spears shivered against the shields. Pridam's shield was pierced, and in his rage he dealt a blow against Galahad's hauberk which would have unseated many a knight.

Again the two drew apart and turned their horses, and they rushed together at a great wallop, so that their spears flew in pieces. Then they dismounted and drew their swords and hacked mightily. Hugh perceived that though Pridam was powerful, he was heavy and slow-footed; whereas Galahad was quick and clear-eyed, and offered many a feint and many a blow, so that Pridam was hard put to avoid them all. And ever Galahad closed in and forced Pridam backward and gave him no rest, until Galahad struck a great blow that carved Pridam's helm apart.

"I yield, sir knight! Have mercy and slay me not!" Pridam cried. And he promised, in return for his life,

never to war on Galahad's lady again, but to aid her in all ways he could.

When the old lady saw that all was lost, she fled back to her own place, and troubled the land no more.

When they came back to the tower, Galahad advised the lady to send for all those who dwelt on the lands about, and he heard them swear fealty to her, and the first to swear was Pridam.

The lady was happier than she had been in many a year, and she would have rewarded them richly, but Galahad would take nothing, nor would Hugh. They thanked the lady for their entertainment, and on the morrow they departed.

As they rode together Galahad said, "Brother, we have righted a wrong. Because you had compassion on the lady for the injustice she suffered, and told me of it, we have achieved this adventure together."

Hugh said, "Things ought not to be so in this land, that a gentlewoman should lose her castle because she has no lord to defend it."

In truth he was thinking of his lady mother; where would she turn if Brannlyr were threatened? Now he knew what she meant when she begged him, "Promise you will return . . . nor leave Brannlyr long without its master."

But Dickon and Tam were stouthearted, he told himself, and the men of the village were loyal; but time was breaching the walls of Brannlyr, and the weapons were rusting in the keep. "Yet you are its lord," Brian had said. "Would you forsake it because you have heard a tale of wonder?"

But the Quest was more than a tale of wonder, and it was happening now; he could not give it up. Yet a little while, and he would go back. One day he would in truth be lord of Brannlyr. So he strove to put down his uneasiness, nor did he speak of it to Galahad.

13

Brother to Galahad

AT EVENING OF THE SECOND DAY Hugh and Galahad
found themselves in a watery woodland crisscrossed by
little streams. Willows leaned athwart the banks and
rooted their branches again in the earth and veiled all
the landscape in yellow-green. Wherever the horses
trod they heard the sucking sound of water beneath the
springing grass, but no other sound, nor was there any
habitation. So they rode on in the greening dusk. In the
midst of the wood they saw a chapel, old and moss-
grown, and there was a stone cross by it.

When they came to it, Galahad checked his horse
and said, "Let us go in."

Hugh dismounted quickly to open the door. Then
he was astonished to see that the door was shut fast,
and that there was neither latch nor handle to it.

Galahad dismounted and said, "Surely there is
some meaning to this mystery. Let us stop here and
mayhap the meaning will be disclosed to us." He did off
his armor and lay down to rest on a stone slab by the
cross.

Hugh slept for a time also. He awoke by full moon-

light and saw the chapel door standing open. Quickly
he arose and entered, and found all dark within. As he
stood there, a pinpoint of light pierced the darkness; it
grew and became a candle flame. Hugh could see the
brass candlestick that held it. The marvel was that nothing supported the candlestick, but it stood of itself in
mid-air. Then an arm came out of the darkness and
grasped the candlestick and bore it across the sanctuary; and above the arm there was nothing. Hugh was
astonished, and watched the moving light, and ere it
vanished it fell on the fair hair of Galahad, who was
kneeling before the altar. Hugh waited by the door, full
of wonder, and he asked Galahad the meaning of what
he had seen.

Galahad answered him, "Verily, Hugh, I saw nothing of it; neither the light nor the candlestick nor the
arm that bore them away."

Hugh was so perplexed he knew not what more to
say. He lay down again, and all that night he pondered
the mystery.

On the morrow they came upon an old man gathering healing herbs in a basket. Galahad dismounted
and greeted him joyfully, for it was Nacien, the holy
hermit. Nacien led them to his dwelling and set food
before them and talked with them concerning the adventure of the Grail. He bade them be steadfast in their
purpose and pass through the Wasteland without fear,

for only by that desolate way could they come to the Castle of Carbonek. As he talked to them of things unseen and still to be, it seemed to Hugh that his wisdom passed that of ordinary men. And Hugh, whose mind was still on the mystery of the chapel, resolved to ask Nacien the meaning of it. Therefore when it came time to go to rest, Hugh stayed and told Nacien the tale and begged to know its meaning.

Nacien answered him, "The meaning is this: you must find your light and follow it."

Hugh asked him, "Why did not Sir Galahad see this thing also?"

"Galahad has ever known his light and followed it," the good man said slowly. "He did not need the vision. But think on this, my son, Galahad's light may not be yours."

Before Hugh could ask him, "What is this light?" there came a knocking at the door. A gentlewoman entered, fair as Queen Guinevere, and she was clad in a nun's habit.

She said, "Reverend father, I seek a knight of King Arthur's court who should pass this way."

Nacien answered, "He is here; he sleeps within."

"God be praised," said the lady, "for I am charged to help him to the high adventure, and the time is near."

When Hugh heard it he hastened to rouse Galahad and help him arm.

The lady said, "Fair sir, we must ride forth with all haste, for the Enchanted Ship draws near with Sir Bors and Sir Percivale already aboard. I shall lead you to the ship and go a little way with you, but not all the way. I am sister to Sir Percivale, therefore this charge was given me."

Galahad answered, "I am ready." He laid his hand on Hugh's shoulder and said, "My kinsman, Hugh of Alleyn, rides with us. He has been both brother and squire to me, and I find him worthy. Therefore lead on, lady, and we will follow."

She mounted her palfrey and they took leave of Nacien and followed her. She rode as fast as her palfrey would carry her until they came to the sea. From the shore they beheld a fair ship speeding toward them over the waves. It was like a ship of some olden time, richly carved and gilded, with hangings and sails of white samite.

"Lady, what manner of ship might this be?" Galahad asked.

"Sir, I will tell you," she answered. "This ship was ordered by King Solomon, and so marvelously wrought that neither wind nor water might harm it. Therein is a rich bed, and the spindles at the head of it were carved from the tree which grew in the Garden of Eden. At the foot of the bed is a sword which belonged to King David, who was Solomon's father. These things the great king prepared for your journey, for you are the last knight of his line."

When she left off speaking, Hugh's mind was besieged with questions, but Galahad asked none. He gazed at the ship and his countenance was joyful as when he spoke of the Grail. Hugh forbore to speak; he watched the ship coming nearer, and felt troubled and all unready. There were things he wished he might do ere the ship bore him away. He would thank Brian for giving him the Thunderer for the journey; he would say his own farewell to Gwynneth and bid her beware of Modred. . . . But heavier things lay deep in his mind, and as the ship drove ever closer they rose to trouble him. How fared his sorrowing mother at Brannlyr? Why had he not sent some word to her? When the Quest was over he would return; he would strengthen the walls and give bread to the poor. . . . Suddenly there was no more time to think. The great ship stood before them; Hugh heard its keel grating on the shore.

Galahad dismounted lightly and raised his shield to it in welcome. From the deck Bors and Percivale called to them and bade them make haste. The lady dismounted and turned her palfrey loose. Galahad took the saddle and bridle from his white horse and loosed him also.

"Now must you find another master," he said.

Then was Hugh's heart heavy out of measure. He had not thought of the horses. His hand stroked the Thunderer's proud neck; his fingers twisted in the beautiful mane, and he felt a pain at his heart. How could he turn away the faithful creature Brian had given him out of friendship?

But Galahad was thinking no longer of the horses; he was full eager to embark. "Let him go, Hugh, we shall not need him more," he said.

Hugh dismounted and stood holding the bridle. "But—Brian gave him to me out of friendship," he said falteringly. "I always thought to give him back when we come again to Camelot. If I let him go now, how shall I find him again?"

Galahad answered him slowly, "Think not of returning, Hugh. When we board the Enchanted Ship we must leave all behind, nor think of returning, ever."

"Not ever? Not ever again?" Hugh asked within himself. The meaing of it came to him slowly and imperfectly; it closed in on his thoughts like the chill of a winter fog; it touched his heart with ice.

"Shall we die then?" he asked in a whisper.

Galahad answered gravely, "Whoso enters the Enchanted Ship weighs not his chances of living or dying. He thinks of naught but the Quest; for it he gladly leaves friends and possessions and all earthly things. And the Grail is the beginning and the end of it; it is his only light."

But Hugh stood mute and despairing. He saw the white sails straining, he heard Bors and Percivale urging them aboard, but something would not let him go.

Galahad perceived it and asked, "What holds you from this adventure, Hugh?"

Suddenly the answer sprang from Hugh's deeper mind, and he heard his words as though another spoke them. "All the things I must finish. All the things I must set right before I sail away forever."

And he knew it was truth, and that he must tell it whole, to himself and to Galahad, while there was time.

Galahad understood and had patience to hear all, and said, "Say on, Hugh, there will be time."

Hugh's words came swiftly, and he reproached himself out of measure. He said, "Though I was lord of Brannlyr, I thought like a child. I wept for shame because it was falling to ruin, and I left it, thinking to win worship in the tournaments at Camelot; nor did I value what my father gave his life to defend. I left my lady mother sorrowing, with no lord to protect her. For that I repent me most of all. Now because of these things I think not first of the Quest, but of our returning, that I might strengthen Brannlyr for the King's service, and feed the poor as the lord ought to do. That I learned at Glaston. And I would keep my oath to follow the King, for in truth I made no other."

"Not even when the vision of the Grail appeared in the hall?" Galahad asked. "Nor when Gawain urged the knights to the Quest?"

Hugh bowed his head in shame. "I did not see the vision," he said. "I saw nothing but the shield. I thought it the fairest thing in the world. I gazed on it so bemused that I could not take my eyes from it, even when others spoke of a greater wonder. When you and Sir Gawain said it was the Grail, I tried to believe I saw it also, but I did not. Now I know it was because I was not worthy of the Quest."

When he had finished speaking, Hugh felt Galahad's hand on his shoulder, and heard him say, "In truth, many who follow it will never be as worthy as you are now, brother."

Hugh looked up in wonder, for he did not understand the saying. Suddenly he saw in Galahad's face all the meaning of knighthood, all that he could ever wish to be, and was not. Then was he overcome with the grief of his new understanding, and he sank to his knees and sought to hide his weeping. And he said, "Sir Galahad, in truth you are the chosen one, and the best knight in the world, and I am all unworthy. Therefore for us the same road must have two endings, as you said. Now

I know the ship waits for you, but not for me. I pray you, before you depart, tell me what I must do."

Then Galahad answered him with gentleness, "Follow your light, as I follow mine. Do good, right wrong, and follow the King."

Then Hugh felt the flat of Galahad's sword strike his shoulder and heard him say, "Rise, Sir Hugh, Knight of Alleyn."

Hugh stumbled to his feet with tears on his face, and such great joy in his heart as made him speechless.

Then Galahad kissed him in full knightly fashion and said, "Fare you well, kinsman and brother, and God go with you, for you too follow the Grail."

Then he trod swiftly through the shallow water and boarded the ship where the lady waited with her

brother and Sir Bors. The white sails filled, and the keel grated on the shingle, and the great ship moved westward. Galahad stood at the rail and raised his arm in farewell. Hugh saw how the light kindled the cross on his shield and cast a halo about his head. So Hugh strained his eyes after the ship that bore the Grail Knight into the sunset. And when the ship was gone beyond sight, and the sunset had burned to ashes, Hugh cast himself down and wept. All the night he stayed there, and heard the gray water lapping the shore like the wake of a great ship passing.

14

Wherein Hugh Meets Launcelot and Tristram

ALL NIGHT HUGH LAY ON THE DISMAL SHORE, lonely in his wakeful dreaming, until Thor nuzzled his shoulder. Then he roused himself and saw that morning lay pale on the water. He rose and mounted the Thunderer, and saw Galahad's horse still standing patiently by. It came when he called it, and followed obediently without a lead rein.

So Hugh turned them from the sea and scanned the landscape for a sign of the way they had come, for he knew Nacien would give him a dole of bread for the journey and point him the way to Camelot. But he had not marked the road in the dark, and so he rode as chance led him. He found no traveled way, nor any dwelling, nor anyone to guide him. After hours of wandering, weariness and hunger rode with him; the night's despair overtook him, and he was cast down out of measure. He reproached himself for his failure, and felt the shame of telling Brian and Gareth how he had fared on the great Quest. And so he wandered until dark, when he came to a ruined tower and a hermit who made it his dwelling.

The hermit was not one who made provision to entertain knights-errant; he was poor and somewhat wandering in his wits, so that he could tell Hugh nothing of the way. But he shared his bread with Hugh, and gave him a dish of boiled lentils, and the horses found sparse grazing by a brook. Early in the morning the old man caught little fish, and broiled them over the coals, and gave them to Hugh with a dole of bread.

So Hugh journeyed until he lost count of the days, but never did he come to the willow-green land where Nacien dwelt, nor did he find anyone who could point him the way to Camelot. The people he met were sorrowful and silent, and when he spoke of King Arthur and Camelot, they looked at him with vacant eyes; yet they shared their food with him, poor though it was. Hugh perceived that the land was dry and parched, and that the trees were stunted and the fruit small and bitter. As he journeyed the land became even poorer, and the people more silent and despairing. Often one would look up from his fruitless toil and, seeing the white horse riderless, point to it and ask, "Where is the one we wait for?"

And when Hugh had no answer for them, they turned away.

The dreary track he followed seemed to have no turning and no end, but grew still more desolate. The rocks were like burnt-out cinders; and after a time the blackened earth offered no food for the horses. Then Hugh knew he must turn back. When he thought of retracing the desolate way he grew sick at heart, and he dismounted and cast himself down to rest. Whether in truth he slept, or fainted from weariness and hunger, he could not tell, but he roused to hear Thor pawing the parched ground and whinnying uneasily beside him. He started to his feet and heard the sound of footsteps on the brittle earth.

So he waited, and at length beheld a knight, partially armed, with a red cloak cast back from his shoulder. Though he walked with weariness, he was powerful and of noble mien. Then Hugh ran to meet him, and fell on one knee before him, and cried out, "Sir Launcelot!"

Launcelot was astonished, and raised him and asked his name.

Hugh answered, "I am Hugh of Alleyn. I served in King Arthur's hall."

"I remember," Launcelot said. "You were squire to my son Galahad."

Launcelot sat down as though for weariness, and rested his head in his hands, and was a long time silent. Then Hugh believed that Sir Launcelot scorned him as a faithless squire, and he was ashamed. He went a little way off, and sat down and thought how he should tell of his parting from Galahad. But when he remembered the knightliness of Galahad he became more unworthy in his own eyes, and he was ashamed to lay his failure before Sir Launcelot.

Yet he had felt the stroke of Galahad's sword on his shoulder, and the greatest knight in the world had called him brother. But he knew that Galahad's parting gift had been given him in trust, against the day when he should accomplish what he had resolved to do. Until then he could not reveal it, not even to Launcelot.

Soon he was aware that Launcelot was watching him, and he went and knelt before him and said, "My lord, I was not faithless to Sir Galahad, though I failed in the Quest. Since he departed on the Enchanted Ship I have wandered uncounted days, nor found a way out of this desolate land. If it be that you return to Camelot, I beg leave to go with you and serve you if I may. I have Sir Galahad's horse yonder, should you have need of him."

Launcelot said, "Right glad I am of that, for in truth I am weary. Do you not know that we are in the Wasteland?"

At that Hugh was astonished and said, "Can this be the Wasteland Nacien told us of—the enchanted land that lies before the Castle of Carbonek?"

"Yea," Launcelot answered. "It is the barren land where people wait to be freed from their desolation by the Grail Knight. But for you and me the great adventure is over, so let us ride hence together."

Then Hugh's spirit lightened because Launcelot did not scorn him. Launcelot perceived it and said, "I have seen my son Galahad and taken my last leave of him, therefore I am heavyhearted."

Then Hugh besought him for news of Galahad, and Launcelot said, "Let us rest here awhile, and refresh ourselves before we take up our journey again, and I will tell you."

So saying, he opened his wallet and filled Hugh's hands with grain. And Hugh, who had been long hungry, ate thankfully. Never had he eaten food so satisfying and so pleasant to the taste. It was both meat and drink to him, and sweeter than honey in the honeycomb, and he marveled what it might be.

Launcelot answered him, "In the burnt-out part of the Wasteland where not even a blade of grass will grow, this grain falls like dew to sustain the faithful who journey in search of the Grail. Methinks it must be like the manna that fell in the wilderness to feed the children of Israel."

Then Launcelot told of his adventure, and how he had wandered until he came to the sea and saw Solomon's ship and boarded it, and so was reunited with his son Galahad. But Bors and Percivale had already left the vessel to seek their adventure by some other way. So Launcelot and Galahad sailed together, with neither pilot nor crew, until they came in sight of an unknown shore. Then a voice bade Galahad take leave of his father and disembark.

And Launcelot said, "So I watched him leave the ship, and on shore a white horse was waiting, all saddled and bridled. Then Galahad mounted and rode off, I know not whither, but I know we shall meet no more in this world."

A sorrowful silence fell upon them as they remembered bright-haired Galahad. Then Hugh said, "I pray you, sir, tell me of your own adventures afterward."

Launcelot said, "When the ship touched land again, I disembarked, and followed a wide, fair road, and at the end of it I saw a castle whose towers and battlements shone white in the moonlight. And as I drew near, two lions barred the way. I drew my sword, but it fell from my hand and clattered on the stones. Then methought I heard a voice say, 'Not by the sword, ye of little faith.'

"So I put up the sword and passed the lions unharmed, and so entered the castle by the postern gate. I found no one within, and all the doors were open, save one. From that place came the fragrance of incense, and the sweetest music that ever I heard, and as I listened I was filled with such peace as to tell of would be past all understanding. Then I knew of a certainty I must be near the Holy Grail. I sought to open the door, but it was fast. Then I prayed that I might be given a sight of that which was within. As if in answer, the door opened, and I heard a voice saying, 'So is your faith rewarded, Launcelot, but come no nearer.' "

Hugh's eyes were fixed on Launcelot's face and he waited, breathless, to hear what lay beyond the open door, while Launcelot paused, calling up the wonder of it.

And Launcelot said, "Such light streamed from that chamber as could scarce be borne by mortal eyes, and in the midst of it I saw the Holy Grail veiled in red samite. A thousand tapers flickered like stars around it, and angels attended it, and meseemed that stars and angels sang together such music as was never heard on earth. The glory of it all was almost too great to be borne, yet in my hardiness I essayed to enter the chamber." Launcelot's voice dropped to a note of wonder. "Then a fiery wind smote me and I fell on the threshold, senseless."

He continued, "When I awoke, Nacien, the holy hermit, was with me, and he told me I was in the Castle of Carbonek, but for my pride and hardiness I should see no more of the Grail."

He added humbly, "Now I understand that my faith was ever in my own strength. I essayed great deeds for love of the Queen, or to win worship in the King's sight. I forgot to do good for its own sake. For me the great adventure is finished; yet I am thankful to have seen so much of its glory."

So saying, he rose, and bade Hugh bring the horses, and said no more concerning his adventure. So they mounted speedily, and set forth, and Launcelot led the way. Now it seemed to them that they passed more quickly through the desolate land, for on the second day their horses ate of the tender grass, and drank from running streams. The travelers dismounted and drank, and washed their hands and faces in the clear water, and on the banks cowslips and violets were coming to bloom.

Launcelot said, "Great fortune it is that we have passed through the burnt-out land so quickly, for I journeyed in it many days."

The next day they passed through a forest and came to a water-meadow whose streams were bordered with willows. In the midst of it was an ancient moss-grown chapel, and the door was open.

When Hugh looked on it he cried, "I passed this way with Sir Galahad! We were in this same chapel."

Thereupon Launcelot reined in his horse and said, "I would go in also."

It was dim and empty as before, moss-covered within as well as without. Hugh knelt on the stone floor beside Launcelot. After a time he seemed to see a pale glow about the altar place, and remembered light falling on the fair hair of Galahad—light from a candle that had appeared to him alone. He marveled anew at the wonder and lost himself in remembrance. Then he was aware of a burst of light and Launcelot startled beside him, and a seven-branched candlestick blazed out of the dark. Transfixed, they watched the burning candles until a hand reached out of the dark and snuffed them out. Then a voice said, "So darkness is falling on the land of Britain."

Launcelot started up and exclaimed, "The King hath need of us!"

So they rode with all speed while daylight lasted, and they came again to the sea.

"Camelot lies south," Launcelot said, and they rode through the swirling mists and the sea-girt cliffs down to a lonely moor. From afar they heard hoofbeats, and an armored knight came riding.

Launcelot spied the device on his shield and cried, "It is Tristram of Lyonnesse!"

Then Hugh remembered the great tournament at Camelot, how Sir Tristram had done most worshipfully in the lists, and won the Queen's ruby and rode away with it to Cornwall.

So the knights met together, and they dismounted and made much of their meeting.

Tristram cried, "Ah, Launcelot, I would lever meet with you than with any man living! Many are on the roads seeking you."

"Why say you so?" Launcelot asked.

Tristram answered, "That you shall hear soon enow. Now let us ride while we may, and lodge tonight at an inn I know of. There I will tell you what hath come to pass in this realm through the workings of Agravaine and Aaron Rheged."

"And Modred?" Hugh spoke the name aloud unwitting.

Tristram looked at him quickly. "Yea, and Modred. They have raised his hopes so high that he surpasses them both in recklessness."

"I marvel to hear it, Sir Tristram," Launcelot said. "I remember when Aaron Rheged brought him to court, a wheyfaced craven whom Hugh here unhorsed before he had even learned to handle a weapon."

"Modred has not yet learned to sit on his horse, yet he aspires to sit on Arthur's throne," Tristram said full scornfully. He remounted swiftly. "Let us ride. The King will have need of us."

15

Wherein Hugh Hears of the End of the Quest

THE INN to which Tristram led them was kept by a knight too old to ride out a-questing. It pleased him therefore to provide food and lodging for traveling knights, for he had good cheer in hearing of their adventures. Right glad he was to see the two most worshipful knights at his table, and he ordered the best meat and drink set before them. When the food was brought, Hugh stood by Launcelot's chair and carved the meat and served the knights as a squire should. Then Launcelot bade him be seated and partake of the meal with them. But Hugh sat a little apart, as was fitting, and ate in silence.

He thought on Tristram's words, and they were past his understanding. In Camelot squires and knights alike had scorned Modred as a weakling—what could have chanced to make the great Tristram take note of him?

Hugh remembered Gwynneth's saying: "Modred casts a shadow on Camelot." It filled him with unease, and he waited for Tristram to tell his tale. But the knights were hungry, and later there would be time for talk.

As they supped, the host came again and said, "One of your fellows, Sir Bors de Ganis, came hither just before you, and lodgeth in a chamber above."

"That is in truth welcome news!" Launcelot exclaimed. Then he said to Sir Tristram, "Bors was with Galahad on the Enchanted Ship."

Tristram said courteously, "I pray you, sir, let send for him. What I have to tell will keep till we ride forth tomorn. Let us ask him concerning our brother Galahad, and of his own fortune on the Quest."

It pleased Launcelot, for he wished mightily to have news of his son. Then Hugh went with the host and told Sir Bors that Launcelot and Tristram were at meat, and Bors made haste to join them. So were three of the greatest knights of the realm met together.

Bors greeted them full courteously and said to Launcelot, "Now indeed is the great Quest accomplished. I salute you for Galahad."

Launcelot bowed his head and said, "Greatly beholden to you for that I am, Sir Bors. I pray you, say on, nor stint to tell all the tale."

Bors answered him, "Sir, I will tell you all, for that I am bounden to do."

Now those at meat thought no more of food, but gave ear to Bors's tale.

And Bors said, "After I left the Enchanted Ship, I wandered much by the way—for how long I cannot tell, since in that land nothing changed and time was not. But on a day I met with Galahad and Percivale again, and we rode together to the Castle of Carbonek. There the people made great joy of our coming, for they had waited long for Galahad. A maiden led us to a chamber where the Fisher King lay on a rich bed, though in great pain. When Galahad drew near, the King knew him, and stretched out his hands to him, and gave thanks. Then was he healed of his pain and his lameness, and his land freed from its old enchantment. Verily, new life came to the Wasteland, and the fresh green spread over it, and the people raised their voices in praise to Galahad, their deliverer."

Hugh and Launcelot heard it with wonder, and looked to one another, remembering how they had marked the greenness spreading into the burnt-out land, nor known the cause of it.

"Then the castle was filled with such joyful music as was never heard on earth," Bors went on.

Tristram was leaning forward, listening. "But the Grail," he said. "Was there in truth a Grail?"

"Can you doubt it?" Bors looked at him amazed.

"I was ever loth to believe a tale of wonder," Tristram said slowly, "and I was not in the hall when the vision appeared. . . . I pray you, say on, Sir Bors."

"I would you had been with us, Sir Tristram," Bors answered, "for I have not tongue to tell the wonders we beheld at Carbonek. We saw a door open, and a procession, methinks of angels, issue forth. One carried the Grail, so bright our eyes could scarce bear the sight of it; another carried a spear; and four bore a throne on which sat a venerable old man clothed like a bishop. They set down the throne by a table inlaid with silver, and on the table they placed the Grail, with candles beside it as it were an altar. We knelt before it and made our prayers, and such was the joy and peace of that place that we wished never to depart from it."

"Happy you are to have known such peace, for there will be no more peace in this land," Tristram said bitterly.

But Bors seemed not to hear, for the Grail music was with him still. Hugh thought suddenly that his countenance was joyous as Galahad's had been whenever he talked of the Quest. But Tristram listened in troubled silence until the tale was done.

And Bors said, "As we knelt together before the Grail I heard Galahad say, 'I thank thee, Lord, that I see what I have so long desired. Now I pray, if it please thee, never let me go from the Grail.'

"When the bishop heard Galahad's prayer, he left his throne and came to Galahad and asked, 'My knight and my true son, know ye who I am?'

"Galahad said, 'Nay, reverend father, I may not know except you tell me.'

"And he said, 'I am Joseph of Arimathea. Our Lord hath sent me here to bear thee fellowship.'

"Then was Galahad filled with joy, for he understood he should have his desire. Then turned he to Percivale, and kissed him and commended him to God. Likewise he came to me and saluted me, and commended me to God, and said, 'Fair lord, salute me to Sir Launcelot, my father, and to my kinsman, Hugh of Alleyn, who took another road, and to my brothers of the Round Table.' "

When they heard it, tears came to the eyes of the knight and squire who loved him best. Bors was silent the while, and Launcelot said, "Sir Bors, tell the tale to the end."

Bors said sorrowfully, "As we continued in prayer, a hand reached down from heaven and caught up the Grail, and so it vanished from our sight. And Galahad's soul departed with it, as he desired, and a flight of angels attended it. Now indeed the great Quest is accomplished, and the memory of it shall be the glory of Britain forever."

"And our brother Percivale—what of him?" Tristram asked.

"He has taken upon him the habit of a monk, and

dwells in a hermitage near Carbonek," Bors answered. "I alone come back to tell the tale."

Then were they silent in sorrow and wonder. Hugh thought on the days when he journeyed with Galahad through the green and pleasant land, and on their leave-taking on the desolate shore, and of all his lonely wandering afterward, and he wept silently that Galahad would not come again.

Then Tristram said, "Happy are you, Sir Bors, and my brothers in chivalry, Sir Launcelot and Hugh of Alleyn, that you followed the Grail with Galahad. Fain would I be numbered with you when men tell of the Quest in the aftertime. My blame it is that I was not in the hall when the vision came to my brother knights."

For it was on that day that Tristram had carried the Queen's ruby to the beautiful Isolde, who was the wife of Mark of Cornwall.

Then Tristram rose from the table and went to his lodging with heavy step. The others sat silent a time, then Launcelot said, "I am greatly beholden to you, Sir Bors, for these tidings. In gratitude I engage me ever to fight at your side in any cause, against any man you call enemy." He raised his head with a flash of his old pride. "In feats of arms I am still Launcelot . . . though now in this realm you stand above us all."

He rose from the table and added, "Now let us

to rest, for tomorn we must ride with all speed to Camelot. Our brother Tristram bears heavy news which you will hear soon enough. Meseems it may in truth foreshadow the dole and sorrow whereof Nimue spoke."

That night Hugh lay long awake, filled with sorrow for the passing of Galahad. Through his grief he seemed to hear the voice of Bors telling the story again. As he followed it in his remembrance, the words became pictures on a marvelous tapestry whereon a thousand candles burned between him and the dark.

He saw Galahad kneeling in red armor, his bright head bowed before the table inlaid with silver, and the heavenly light streaming from the Grail. A venerable bishop raised his hand in blessing, and Hugh knew him for Joseph of Arimathea. Then he saw Galahad rise to salute Percivale and Bors, and heard him say, "Salute me to my kinsman, Hugh of Alleyn, who took another road."

And suddenly Hugh saw himself in his rust-colored tunic, standing with Bors and Percivale. He saw Galahad turn to him smiling, and heard him say: ". . . for you too follow the Grail."

The picture faded, but the meaning of it spoke to Hugh's deeper mind: For you too follow the Grail— by another road.

Then doubt made him answer, "How can that be, since the great Quest is over?"

Out of Hugh's memory of Glaston, the good Abbot Walterius spoke: "Should not each man in his own time have a vision and a quest to follow?"

From the willow-green land Nacien, the holy hermit, answered: "Yea, and think on this, my son—Galahad's light may not be yours."

Then Hugh perceived a truth as clear as the light from the Grail: Each man has his own quest to follow —one thing he must achieve above all else. That is his light and his grail; it is his and no other's.

He had not wholly failed. For had he not glimpsed his light on the dismal shore by the Enchanted Ship? Now he knew for certain that his own quest was still before him. Galahad had known it too, and called him brother. Brother to Galahad! He was no longer alone, nor overwhelmed with sorrow. A feeling of peace swept over him, and so at last he slept.

16

The Treachery of Modred

EARLY ON THE MORROW King Arthur's men made them ready to depart. When they were gathered at table the host himself brought in a steaming haggis of chopped mutton and meal boiled together in a tripe. As they ate, Sir Tristram told his tale.

He said, "My brothers, you have followed marvelous adventure in a land where time was not. But in this land the seasons passed one into another; and as each passing season fades in its glory, so is fading the former glory of this realm."

The listeners heard him in amazement. Bors half rose in his place but forbore to speak. Hugh felt dismay and something of anger; he wanted to challenge Tristram's words, to say it could not be, but he kept silent. Launcelot's fist struck the table like a command, and Tristram went on.

"After the last tournament I rode into Cornwall to the court of my uncle Mark. That was not long after Sir Launcelot had put down Magdelant of Albany, whose lands lie close to the border of Cornwall. There I learned that Aaron Rheged and Agravaine were in

Albany, with a strong force of pagans from the north—Picts and out-islanders who revere not King Arthur. When I heard of this I made excuse to tarry in Cornwall to learn their purpose, and Dinadan went into Albany to spy among Magdelant's people.

"The Cornishmen declared to me that Aaron Rheged came often to Albany and encouraged Magdelant to harry them and seize their lands, and used his Pictish warriors to stir up strife on the borders. And the reason for it was that the people might weary of warfare and say that Arthur could not keep peace in the realm. And ever and anon Aaron went among them saying that Modred would be a better king than Arthur."

"Treason!" Launcelot's fist crashed down on the table and set the cups and plates rattling. "Methought Aaron was out of his wits when he sought to have Arthur name that lily-livered Modred to be King after him. Has it come to this—that he would have Modred king while Arthur lives?"

"Even so," said Tristram angrily. "Arthur knows there is nothing of worship in Modred, though he is Arthur's sister's son. Nay, he is all Rheged, cowardly and treacherous, though with a vaingloriousness he passes off for courage. And because Arthur will not grant Rheged's suit, Rheged plots to bring it about in his own way."

"Think you aught can come of this folly?" Bors asked scornfully.

"You name it lightly, Sir Bors," Tristram said shortly. "Methinks Sir Launcelot came closer to the truth. For Dinadan brought word that Agravaine has gone across the Channel to seek the aid of Claudas."

"He doeth shame to the Order of Knighthood!" cried Bors.

"It is pity that he liveth," Launcelot said, and his anger was terrible and just.

The name of Claudas stabbed Hugh like a spear-thrust. Pain tightened his chest and shattered his breath. He sprang to his feet and the words choked out of him: "Arthur is king!" His voice broke off as he strove to say it again. "Arthur . . ." He caught his breath, his voice steadied and fell lower. "Arthur is king!"

"Yea, and we will make it good with our lives!" Bors answered him.

"To horse!" Launcelot commanded them. His hand fell on Hugh's shoulder. "Brother of my son Galahad, you will ride with me."

So they mounted, and rode toward Camelot with all speed. As they journeyed back into the world of men they perceived that the summer had fled before them. The fields of the earth-men were stripped of their harvest and lay dun-colored in the pale sun. Their cottages were shut and banked with earth and straw against the coming cold.

Along a desolate road a man came riding and when he saw the company he shouted and spurred forward. It was Sir Lavaine.

Lavaine said, "Praise be that I have found you, Sir Launcelot, though it grieveth me to be the bearer of heavy tidings."

"What tidings, Sir Lavaine?" Launcelot asked.

"Of double woe that springs from a single cause," Lavaine answered. "Modred is in open revolt and has challenged Arthur for the crown. In the first skirmish Modred was put to flight, but Sir Gawain was sore wounded . . . nay, his wound was mortal. . . ." Lavaine turned away his eyes and searched his wallet.

Launcelot was silent as though he had not heard. Then he said heavily, "Sir Gawain fallen! I made him knight. No man living was dearer to me."

Lavaine drew forth a letter and offered it to Launcelot. "He wrote it ere he died, and charged me to put it in your hands," he said.

The others waited in silence while Launcelot broke the seal and read:

> *Unto Sir Launcelot, flower of all noble knights that ever I knew or heard of in all my days, I, Sir Gawain, King Lot's son of the Orkneys, sister's son*

*to the noble King Arthur, send greeting. Know that
on the same day that I write this letter, I was smitten
upon an old wound and hurt to the death, in battle
against the false traitor Modred.*

*Now I beseech you, Sir Launcelot, to make no
tarrying, but to come in haste with your men at arms
and rescue the noble King who made you knight, for
he is sore beset. And I entreat you, for the knightly
love that was between us, to visit my tomb and pray
for my soul.*

Launcelot was silent a time; then he folded the letter
and said, "Heavy to bear is the loss of our brother Gawain. It shall not go unrequited. Gentle Lavaine, tell
us how Modred moved in this treason, and where we
may search him out."

Lavaine answered, "When Modred saw his hope of
the kingdom slipping away, he besought Arthur to make
him ruler over Albany and Cornwall at least. But the
Cornishmen sent to Arthur saying they would in no
wise have Modred over them. When Modred heard it,
he went into Cornwall with the Picts and Magdelant's
men and laid all waste, and left not one stone upon another, nor so much as would sustain a fly. And men
from Southsex and Eastsex, and from Northfolk and
Southfolk drew unto Modred by reason of Aaron's per-
suasion, and some from Kent and Surrey, who were
fickle and eager for change. With these Modred came
out against Arthur, and challenged him for the king-

dom. We went out against them and drove Modred to Barham Down, and there it misfortuned Gawain to be stricken."

When they heard Lavaine's tale, Arthur's men were aghast at treason that recked not for kinship nor knightly oath; and they feared for the safety of the King and the realm.

Launcelot said, "Sir Tristram, at feats of arms we two are matched. For the love we bear the King, I charge you, take my place by his side in the field until I come. Hugh, go with Sir Tristram as my messenger. Say to the King that I go with all speed to my father's castle at Benwick to summon up his knights. If Claudas essays to cross into Britain, neither he nor his men will ever walk on dry land again. Bors, my kinsman, hasten to my castle, Joyous Gard, and take my knights to Arthur. So shall we root out this treachery."

So saying, he bade them Godspeed, and turned toward the sea, that he might take ship.

And Bors said, "Hugh, salute me also to my lord King Arthur, and say that I will come with all haste. Tell him how our brother Galahad achieved the Quest of the Holy Grail, for that will be a light to him against the darkness of Modred's treachery." So Bors departed toward Joyous Gard.

Now Hugh and Tristram had not ridden but a mile or two when they met a herald named Cerdic, who had

Brother to Galahad

been sent forth to summon Arthur's knights. Cerdic told them of the knights who had lately returned from the Quest—among them Lucan and Bedivere and Kay the Seneschal—and he told of those he had met by the way and sent to join the King. And Cerdic said that the King was camped with his host westward toward Salisbury, and thither Hugh and Tristram rode with all speed.

When they were come nigh the place they saw the encampment from afar, and in the midst of it the King's tent, and knights and squires and yeomen in companies. And it was not far from the circle of ancient stones where Hugh had sworn his hand-fast oath to Arthur because Aaron and Modred were riding to Camelot. It came to him that time had swung a full mysterious circle and brought him to that place again, and whether it was an end or a beginning he knew not.

When Hugh and Tristram were come to the encampment they passed by the outer guards and through the press of warriors and horses, and came upon Sir Lucan and Bedivere. They alighted from their horses and gave charge of them to a groom, and went with Bedivere to the King.

Hugh knelt before the King and said, "My lord Arthur, I salute you for Sir Bors de Ganis and Sir Launcelot of the Lake. They will come with all speed to the King's aid, bringing the knights of Benwick and

Joyous Gard. And Sir Bors bade me say that the Quest of the Holy Grail was indeed accomplished by Sir Galahad, who charged him to salute the King and his brethren in his name."

"And Galahad?" the King asked.

"He will not come again, my lord. His soul departed with the Grail," Hugh answered.

When the King heard it, sorrow shadowed his countenance and he said, "Alas, Sir Galahad! So late he joined our fellowship, and so soon departed! In all this world there was not his equal. I grieve for his passing as I grieve for my kinsman Gawain. But treason is on the march, and leaves us no time to mourn this double sorrow."

He turned to Tristram and said, "Sir Tristram, Modred marches toward Salisbury Plain with a hundred thousand men. Think you we should wait Launcelot's reinforcements here, or move now to some more advantageous ground where we may make a stand?"

Tristram answered, "My lord, advance to Camlan and wait Modred there. So you will shorten the distance between yourself and Launcelot. And mayhap you can take Modred unaware and strike the first blow."

But the King shook his head and said, "Nay, Sir Tristram, I am loth to make war on my own kindred. I will not strike first."

"My lord, he is but a traitor!" Tristram cried. "I would cut him down as I would cut down a snake fanged to strike!"

"Yet I must essay to treat with him once more," the King said. "I will offer goods and lands to sway him from this madness."

"My lord, I have not your nobleness," Tristram said. "But if you must parley with this traitor, offer him what lands and goods you will, but move slowly and delay as long as you can, so shall we gain time until Bors and Launcelot join their forces with yours. Then, my lord, if Modred will not make peace, he shall learn how the King's knights make war."

The plan pleased the King, and he moved his forces to Camlan. There they set up their tents and dug trenches and raised earthworks about the encampment. On the third day Hugh found Brian. The two friends made much of their meeting; Brian and the Thunderer made much of each other also, and Hugh was afoot again. Gareth greeted Hugh and asked him many things concerning his adventure, but Gareth was not merry as of old, and Hugh knew he sorrowed for the loss of his brother Gawain. After that Hugh was much with the young knights and served them both as squire, and Tristram rode always with the King.

17

The Passing of Arthur

THEY HAD BEEN BUT A FEW MORE DAYS at Camlan when Bors came from the south with the knights of Joyous Gard, and their numbers heartened the King. He deployed his men by companies, knights and yeomen, and found among them many who at first held with Modred and turned again, and followed the King. So the warriors made their battle preparations as Bors and Tristram and Bedivere commanded them. And Hugh went back and forth to the armorers' forges with weapons and armor for Gareth and Brian; Tristram sent him hither and yon with messages to Bors and Bedivere; Lucan the Butler set him to stirring the cooking pots and serving the knights. So Hugh became messenger and squire and scullion again, when he would fain be a fighting man.

Then on a day one of the King's spies came riding with all speed, saying that Modred was nigh with a host of a hundred thousand. Toward evening they saw the banners and pikes of the enemy moving into the plain. Now Tristram besought the King to haste into battle and seize the advantage while Modred's men were weary. But the King refused, saying he would never be the first to shed the blood of a kinsman, nor to loose hateful war in his own realm.

When the King had gone to his tent, Lucan the Butler summoned Hugh to serve the King's supper, for Gryflet the squire was busy readying his lord's weapons and armor. Lucan ordered Hugh to remain in the King's pavilion and take his squire's place as long as the King had need of him. So it was that when the torches were lighted Hugh was in the King's tent with Bedivere the Cupbearer. And Hugh looked up and saw a man clad in black with a green cloak cast back from his shoulder. He went and stood before the King, nor knelt to do him homage. Though his hair was gray, he stood straight as a young man, and in the torchlight his strange eyes glittered green and brown!

Hugh caught his breath and stood stone-still in his place. The King rose full pale and said, "Speak, Merlin!"

And Merlin said, "My lord Arthur, the time has come full circle. Now I must depart this middle earth and sleep beneath the ancient stones I raised when this land was new. In those days a greater race of men lived under the sun. I taught their wise men to talk with eagles and ravens, and to read the future in the wheeling planets. Out of my wisdom I devised the Round Table and the Order of Knighthood, and in due time I laid on thy knights the Oath of Chivalry. Now the noble fellowship of the Round Table is broken forever. So must I go from this realm until the time when I shall order the Round Table anew. For wit you well, all that the Round Table signifieth shall never pass from this land, nor shall evil prevail against true knighthood."

The King said, "Merlin, ere you depart, what is your counsel?"

Merlin answered, "This last warning I give thee, O King, that ye in no wise do battle with Modred to-morn. An ye do, ye shall surely be slain, and many other good men beside. Rather make a treaty with him for a month and a day. Spare not, but offer him lands and goods as largely as ye must to delay. For soon Sir Launcelot will come to your aid. Even now he is destroying the forces of your enemy Claudas on the Channel beach. If ye escape battle tomorn, ye shall have the victory."

So saying, Merlin passed from the King's presence.

All that night Hugh was wakeful, ready to serve if the King summoned him. He pondered on Merlin's fateful warning, and he was restless for daybreak. He rose while it was yet dark and went to the tent door and pushed the tapestry aside. Gray clouds rolled across the sky and curled their edges like waves breaking over middle earth; beneath them the dawn flamed saffron and red. Crimson streaks overshot the gray-purple clouds and mingled with them, yet without brightness. It seemed to Hugh that fire and darkness contended together to overwhelm the world of men. As he watched, one came and stood beside him; Hugh saw it was the King.

Hugh knelt and greeted him courteously and would have withdrawn, but the King restrained him and said, "Nay, let us watch this fateful dawn together. If fortune favor us, we shall live to see the sunset."

But then came Tristram and Lucan and Bedivere, and they took counsel with the King. As soon as it was light, Arthur sent Lucan and Bedivere to treat with Modred, and offer gifts for a truce. They parleyed with Modred above two hours, and returned saying that Modred would accept the land of Kent for a truce of a month and a day. And it was agreed that Modred and the King should talk together at a place betwixt the armies, and that both sides should lay down their arms while they talked.

To all this the King agreed, and he called for horse and made ready to ride out. Sir Tristram distrusted Modred, and begged to ride at the King's side. But the agreement was that only Lucan and Bedivere should attend him, so the three rode forth and Hugh and Tristram went out and watched them depart. Then Tristram went among the host and Hugh with him. Tristram charged them to keep strict watch on Modred's men;

if anyone should see even a single sword raised, that one should cry the alarm. And Tristram charged them: "If you hear the alarm, let every man rush on fiercely, and slay all before him, and rescue the King."

And on Modred's side the heralds cried like warning.

While the parley went on Hugh sat among the King's men on the heath, and a little way off a young warrior sat at his ease, waiting. A little adder came out of a bush, and Hugh saw it slip over the ground toward the man. Swiftly it raised its head and darted out its tongue, and stung the man on the hand. The warrior looked down and saw the serpent and drew his sword to slay it. Straightway those on both sides saw the sword and cried the alarm. Then rose the din of war trumpets and hunting horns, and the grim shouts of warriors on both sides as they rushed into battle.

Hugh leaped to his feet and strove to avoid the press of men and horses. Fain would he have ridden with them, but he had neither horse nor arms. He saw the King turn and ride swiftly toward his own men, and Lucan and Bedivere with him. As the battle tide surged on, the King turned again and rode at its head into the most doleful war that ever came to any land.

Hugh ran swiftly to the top of an ancient barrow that overlooked the plain, and he saw the armies clash in a fierce medley. Knights rushed over the field thrust-

ing and striking down without asking or giving mercy. Never were so many mortal strokes given in so short a space; never were so many noble knights so quickly cast to earth. It seemed to Hugh that he had deserted the King and the knights he loved because he watched the deadly fighting from a barrow. It came to his mind that he might get arms from the armorers' tents, mayhap a horse, and ride forth to do what he might. And yet his charge was to serve in the King's pavilion. What if the King were brought wounded from the field, and he was not there? He could not forget Merlin's warning, nor his fear for the King's life. So he stayed and watched for a sight of the King's crimson plumes as Arthur rode fearlessly wherever the tide of battle took him. From the first onrush the fighting grew ever fiercer. Dust rose above the tumult until it hid the battlefield and dimmed the sun, and the shouting, thundering battle noise seemed to fill middle earth.

Thus they fought all the day long, and never slackened until it was near night. And all that day Hugh stayed on the barrow. At evening he saw King Arthur and Lucan and Bedivere riding out of the battle haze. He gave a shout of triumph at the sight of them. His day-long fear was swept away in joy for the King's safety. The old Enchanter's prophecy had failed. Merlin should have known that the shield-wall of Arthur's knights would protect the King from his enemies. Merlin was an old man, and no warrior; he could not know the might of Arthur and Launcelot and Tristram of Lyonnesse. Surely, then, Merlin was no true Enchanter. So Hugh thought as he raced down the barrow. Then he saw how Sir Lucan slumped in the saddle and carried his shield low, and Hugh knew that he was wounded. Bedivere helped him to dismount and led him to shelter.

Hugh waited for the King to command him, but the King turned and looked back to the battlefield, and his grief was very great. The dust was settling over the doleful scene, and a hundred thousand lay dead on the plain.

The King said, "Alas, my brother knights, you have served this realm full nobly; full sorrowful I am of your deaths." So the King took no thought of himself, but grieved out of measure for his knights wounded and slain.

Hugh said, "My lord, my father perished at the siege of Brannlyr, and afterward I had this saying from Herlewin the Chaplain: 'Let us not call his passing death, for who can die while Britain lives?' "

The King laid his hand on Hugh's shoulder and said, "Gramercy, Hugh. It is a brave saying, and true. I will hold it in my own remembrance."

Then they saw a man, without armor, walking alone on the battlefield. He stopped and rested on his sword, and looked about him. And both Hugh and the King knew it was Modred.

The King's anger rose at the sight of him, and he cried, "Now give me my spear again, for there stands the traitor who brought this woe to the realm!"

Bedivere was returning and he heard and cried out, "My lord Arthur, I beseech you, remember Merlin's warning and forbear! So far the King has been spared and we hold the field. Only let this fatal day pass, and in truth you shall be revenged. For this night at least, let the traitor be!"

But the King answered, "Betide me life or death, he shall not escape me; I shall never have him at better avail!"

So saying, he gripped his spear in both hands and rushed toward Modred shouting, "Traitor, your life is ended!"

When Modred heard it, black rage bereft him of his wits, and he ran toward Arthur with his sword drawn in his hand. The King's spear point did not stop him; he rushed on it with such force that it thrust him through the body. Modred knew he had his death wound, but his rage was so great that he thrust himself still forward, even to the bur of King Arthur's spear. Thus, with his sword gripped in both hands, Modred smote the King. The keen blade cut through the King's helmet and dealt a mortal blow.

When Hugh and Bedivere saw Modred's upraised
sword they leapt on horse—Hugh on Lucan's—and
spurred to the King; but they could not prevent the fatal
stroke. They saw the noblest of kings fall wounded,
and Modred dead on Arthur's spear. They did what
they could to aid the King, and stayed by him until
he opened his eyes. When they essayed to raise him,
he besought them to take him to the sea. Bedivere urged
him to let them fetch someone to dress his wounds, but
the King would not; he entreated them to make haste

and take him to the water's edge. With much care they got him on horse, for he was too weak to stand. As they carried the wounded King from the battlefield, their hearts were heavy with foreboding.

Slow and sad was the journey, and the King suffered great pain, but always he urged them to the sea. They came at last to the steel-gray shore, fog-shrouded and silent, save for the sighing sea grasses and the moaning tide and the mourning sea birds wheeling out of the ghostly mist. In such a place Avallach, Prince of Evening, might have ruled among the shades, or Finn Lug dwelt with the water gods of Avalon. There they saw a ruined chapel, and to it they carried the wounded King. They laid him down on Bedivere's cloak and they knew not what else to do.

The King opened his eyes and said, "The time for departure is near. Sir Bedivere, take my good sword Excalibur and go swiftly and cast it into the water. Come with all haste again and tell me what you have seen."

Bedivere took the sword, and its blade was of Baltic steel and its pommel heavy with jewels set in gold; his hand tightened on the ivory haft of it, and he went out swiftly. Hugh stayed by the King until Bedivere came again.

Bedivere said, "My lord, I went to the shore and

cast away the sword. I saw nothing but the waves; I heard nothing but the wind."

The King said, "Alas, that you should so deceive me, Bedivere. Go with all speed and cast it in, or I shall have my death."

Bedivere went a second time, and came again and said, "My lord, I cast away the sword, and I saw nothing but the sea birds; I heard nothing but the tide."

The King roused and spoke sternly, with majesty in his look. "Am I not still king, Bedivere? You were my companion at arms and my cupbearer in the hall. Would you betray me now for the richness of my sword?"

The knight bowed his head in shame. "Forgive me, my lord; this time I will not fail." To Hugh he said, "Stay by the King until I come."

Then the King began to sorrow for his land and people and said, "Alas, that I must depart this realm when all I strove to accomplish is undone. Dole and strife lie heavy on the land; my knights are fallen in battle or gone away to their own countries, and the noble fellowship of the Round Table is broken forever."

Hugh sought to comfort him, and knelt beside him and said, "My lord, remember Merlin's saying, 'All that the Round Table signifieth shall never pass from this land, nor shall evil prevail over true knighthood.' "

"Yea," the King answered, "they were true to their knighthood, the men of the Round Table, and truest and noblest of all was Galahad."

At the name of Galahad Hugh bowed his head in double sorrow.

And the King mused, "Greatest of all knightly quests was his, the greatest that shall ever be in this world. Mayhap in the aftertime men will say, 'These things were accomplished in the time of Arthur—the ordering of the Round Table and the Quest of the Holy Grail.' " As the King thought on it he smiled, and was comforted.

Then came Bedivere in haste and cast himself on his knees by the King and said, "My lord Arthur, in very truth I cast the sword out over the water, and it cut through the mist like light. As it fell, an arm clothed in white came up out of the water and caught it, and brandished it thrice in the air and drew it under."

The King said, "Now bear me to the water's edge and wait with me there."

When they were come to the water's edge the mist was still cleft by Arthur's sword, and they saw a black barge coming over the water bearing a company of ladies fair as queens, and all robed in black. Their voices came over the tide in sorrowful lament for King Arthur.

As the barge touched the shore the King said, "It comes for me. I pray you, lift me on board."

They lifted him as gently as they could, and laid him down on a fur robe. The fairest lady of all took his head in her lap and said, "Dear brother, why tarried ye so long?" And all the ladies wept for the wounded King.

Then Bedivere cast himself on his knees and burst into weeping and said, "Fair ladies, I beseech you, tell me, what betokens this mourning and lament?"

The King said, "Grieve not, Bedivere, for I must leave this realm and pass to the Island Vale of Avalon to be recovered of my wound. Concerning this passing, Hugh hath a true saying—'who can die while Britain lives?'"

And Hugh, weeping, said, "My lord, the name of Arthur shall not die while Britain lives."

The saying pleased the King, and he smiled and signed them farewell. They went on shore and watched as the barge sailed toward the sunset Vale of Avalon. Ever the sorrowful lament of the queens drifted back over the tide, and Hugh and Bedivere wept together over the passing of Arthur.

18

The End and the Beginning

On the morrow Sir Bedivere resolved to take on him the life of a hermit and abide in that chapel the rest of his days. He charged Hugh to go to Queen Guinevere and tell her of the passing of her lord King Arthur. Hugh promised, and took leave of Bedivere and rode for Camelot.

As he turned from the bleak shore he thought of the roses and fountains of many-towered Camelot, of ladies in trailing silks and jeweled slippers, of pages singing of love and death and summertime, of Queen Guinevere walking with Sir Launcelot. To him they were like figures in a tapestry woven of his own long-gone dream. He remembered Gwynneth's saying: "a wall of shining air shuts us away from the other world." Since then Hugh had journeyed far and he understood the saying better. He knew the other world held wastelands as well as gardens, wars as well as tournaments, and quests that could never be achieved. There a knight could test his strength and win no ruby prize—but mayhap some other prize that was for him alone. Hugh could not put it clearly to himself, and he tried to give over thinking of it. But the towers of Brannlyr rose out of his thought of the other world; he saw them as once he had seen the towers of Camelot. The ancient battlements were still strong, and he was its lord. Now he would go back and do the things he had left undone— all he had resolved to do on the shore by the Enchanted Ship. He was ready for his own quest at last. His heart lifted at the thought. Again he rode with Galahad.

When he came near to Camlan, the place where the dolorous battle was fought, he saw a knight on horse, and it was Brian on the Thunderer. Brian was riding to Camelot, heavyhearted for his brother knights wounded and slain. As they rode together, Brian told how Launcelot came too late, and disbanded his knights and sent them to their own realms again, and went to Camelot alone. Hugh told of the passing of Arthur, and how Bedivere resolved to take on him the life of a hermit.

Brian said sadly, "What else is left for us, since our King is departed and our fellowship scattered? Meseems I knew more of contentment in the forest of Brannlyr than ever I found at Camelot. Perchance I shall return to my hut and my bees, and so live out my days. And yet, how shall I forget Arthur and the Table Round?"

Hugh cried, "We must never forget Arthur! Though I was but a little while in Camelot, and served in the kitchen and did no knightly deeds, I knew the nobleness of Arthur and his knights, and I would tell it to the men of Brannlyr! I would build our walls to defend his realm, and have the youths train for his knighthood. I would take thought for my people and give bread to the poor—so I promised my brother Galahad. These things I fain would do, but I know not how to begin. Sir Brian, you were in truth a knight of the Round Table; I beseech you, help me order these things at Brannlyr that men may remember the King!"

As Brian listened his look grew eager, and some of the sadness left him, and he said, "Yea, let us essay it together! Let us gather others of our fellowship, and the young knights, Ector and Gryflet and Dinadan. Mayhap we shall raise another Camelot—at Brannlyr!"

So their hearts were lightened, and they rode with purpose and dispatch for Camelot. There Brian went to spread the word among the knights, while Hugh waited for admittance at the porter's gate.

Queen Guinevere was by the fountain conversing with Sir Launcelot. Gwynneth stood by with a furred cloak, for the sun was pale and chill. There was no rainbow in the fountain, and all the roses were fallen. Gwynneth saw Hugh first and she started as though she would speak, but held silence before the Queen, and welcomed him with her look.

Hugh knelt and saluted the Queen and Sir Launcelot and said, "Sir Bedivere, the King's Cupbearer, sent me hither as his messenger. He will not come again to Camelot, for he has chosen to live all his days as a hermit in a ruined chapel that sheltered the King. Therefore he charged me to tell our lady the Queen how King Arthur departed this realm."

When the Queen had given him leave, Hugh haltingly told the tale. He said much of Bedivere's care of the wounded King, but of his failure with the sword he said nothing, for he knew Bedivere repented it, and loved the King well. And then Hugh told of the sunset voyage to Avalon. Guinevere bowed her shining head and the bright tears fell down as she wept for her lord King Arthur. Gwynneth laid the cloak over the Queen's shoulders and her own eyes filled with tears for the passing of the King and the grief of the Queen.

Launcelot strove to hide his own sorrow and comfort the Queen, and he said, "My lady, some there be who hold that Arthur cannot die, but passeth to the Island Vale of Avalon, to come again and rule this land once more."

But the Queen was not comforted and said, "I wist not if this tale be true; I only know the King is gone. For me this realm holds no more of joy. So shall I betake me to the convent of Almesbury and dwell there while my life lasts, and pray for the soul of my lord King Arthur and this unhappy land."

Sir Launcelot made answer, "My lady, had it been your wish to abide in Camelot, I would gather my knights again and serve you all my days, as I would have served the King. But if you would in truth withdraw from the world . . ."

The Queen said, "Yea, Sir Launcelot, that is my desire."

"Then I will go to Glastonbury with my kinsman Bors, and we will dwell among the brethren there," Launcelot said. "For our old companions are gone—Gawain first, then his brother Gareth at Camlan. The mighty Tristram is wounded and gone to Cornwall to be healed. Bedivere and Percivale will not come again, nor Galahad, my son. In the aftertime our fellowship may rise anew, but other knights will sit at the Table. They will remember us, and at their high feasts they will tell our story and rehearse the knightly deeds of Arthur.

"Hugh, let this be your charge, to tell men of his dream for this realm—peace with justice and law."

"That I am sworn to do, my lord!" Hugh answered. "I go first to tell it to the men of Brannlyr."

The Queen said, "Gramercy, fair youth, for your faithfulness. In happier times I would have named you among my knights, for I find you worthy."

Launcelot answered, "Worthy he is, my lady, and knight already. Galahad conferred on him the honor of knighthood, but he made no mention of it and served humbly as before. Yet he was true to his own knightly oath and followed the King to the end. One last reward I can give him. . . ."

Launcelot took a golden spur from his sword belt and held it in his hand. "One spur I gave to Galahad," he said. "The other I kept for remembrance."

Swiftly he knelt and fixed the spur to Hugh's heel. "Sir Hugh, you have earned your golden spur," he said. "May you prosper in your quest." And Hugh rose, and Launcelot clasped his arm and saluted him in knightly fashion, and so they took leave of each other.

Launcelot and the Queen departed, but Gwynneth stayed. She held out her hands and said, "You are welcome, Sir Hugh."

Glad were they both of their meeting, but as they talked Hugh was still mindful of the Queen's purpose, and he could not forbear to ask, "Gwynneth, what will you do when the Queen goes to the cloister?"

She answered quickly, "I will go also."

"But—not to remain?" Hugh questioned.

Gwynneth nodded without speaking.

"You mean—forever?" Hugh had not thought of that. "But Gwynneth, is that in truth your wish?"

"Where else can I go?" Gwynneth's eyes misted with tears, and she turned her face away. "If our hall still stands in Cornwall, could I dwell there alone? If any of Modred's followers still live to wreak his vengeance on Cornwall, think you they would spare Cormac's daughter?"

Cormac! The name astonished Hugh to silence. Then came the swift remembrance of his vigil at Brannlyr, of the bowed figure of the once-proud chieftain of Cornwall. He remembered the silvery hair falling over the scarred cheek, and the eyes shadowed by past suffering. Wonder held him silent as he strove to order his thoughts.

Gwynneth was looking at him, waiting for him to speak. He heard himself asking, "Was your father indeed called Cormac?"

She answered proudly, "My father was Cormac, Chieftain of Cornwall. He rode out against King Claudas and came not back, as I told you."

"Yea, you told me, but you did not name him!" Hugh said. "Our fathers fought together in that battle. The valiant Cormac was not slain, but grievously wounded. Gwynneth, your father lives at Brannlyr!"

Gwynneth's tears fell as Hugh told all the tale, and when it was finished she said, "If I could but look on his face again, I would never see the scars!"

"In truth you would not, nor did I at the last," Hugh said slowly. Then a thought came to him and he said, "Lady Gwynneth, ride with us to Brannlyr! You can dwell there with your father. My lady mother will welcome you, for she is often lonely and fain would have a daughter to bear her company. And Moira will attend you, for she gave me up long ago, and she will tell you tales of spirits and old water-gods whenever the fog comes down!"

"I love the fog," Gwynneth said softly, and she smiled a little through her tears.

"There is often fog at Brannlyr," Hugh said. "It rises from the sea, and there are cliffs, as at Cornwall." He looked at Gwynneth anxiously, trying to think of something else to offer.

She said softly, "My father is there! That is enough. I will go, if your lady mother . . ."

A loud wail came from the shrubbery, and little Lady Vivien burst forth, drowned in tears. "Do not go and leave me!" she cried. "I have no other home. What shall I do here if everyone goes away?" She clung to Gwynneth, sobbing, and would not be comforted.

But Sir Hugh remembered a knight's obligation to a damsel in distress. He said, "Why then, we will surprise my lady mother with two daughters."

Saint Martin's summer came in a tide of golden warmth to the autumn land. It touched the fields with ocher and gilded the last leaves and brought the small wood-creatures out of their burrows into the sun. Dry leaves crackled beneath the horses' hoofs, rabbits froze in their tracks, and white-tailed deer vanished in a trice before the pack train that wound through the woods.

Brian and Hugh rode at the head, with Gwynneth and Vivien just behind. After them came mules bearing weapons and armor, with Gryflet and Ector following. Hugh looked at the towering trees, copper beech and spreading oak. He could well be proud of the forest of Brannlyr. Somewhere near them ran the little stream where he used to fish with Tam. Brian raised his hand and pointed to a tethered horse. Behind them Vivien was exclaiming shrilly over a rabbit.

A youth stepped out of a thicket with a fish net in his hand. He was stout and red-faced, and he looked at the travelers curiously.

"Tam!" Hugh shouted, and reined in his horse.

Tam dropped the net and stared. Then he ran forward and dropped on one knee by Hugh's stirrup.

"Welcome home, young master . . . my lord," he corrected himself in embarrassment.

Hugh reached down his hand and Tam rose awkwardly.

"Tam, how fares my lady mother?"

"She is in health," Tam answered. "She will rejoice at your coming." He added eagerly, "I have a fast horse, my lord. Shall I go ahead and tell the village you are come?"

"Yea, go to my mother. . . . But wait!" Hugh

saw how Gwynneth was leaning forward, listening. He turned to her.

"I want to be the one to tell him," she said, and joy lighted her face.

Hugh nodded and turned to Tam again. "Ride on and give your news. Go to my mother first. Then bid Dickon make room for the horses and mules. Tell the villagers there will be bread, and work mending the walls."

Then Tam was gone, galloping his horse over the forest track. The others quickened their pace, and their thoughts outran them. They rode the last mile in silence.

Near the edge of the wood the towers of Brannlyr suddenly overtopped the trees. Hugh looked up at them and felt pride in their rugged strength. He had not remembered them so high. He checked his horse at the clearing, and, even as he gazed, two flags ran up on the towers that flanked the barbican. His mother's welcome! He felt a thrill of pride, and a tightening in his throat.

Brian laid a hand on Hugh's arm. "It is a fit homecoming, Sir Hugh," he said. "Brannlyr welcomes its lord."

Gwynneth reined in beside him. She was smiling, and her blue eyes were bright. "You did not tell me all of it," she said. "It is as beautiful as Camelot."